OUTBACK LILY

episodes from a to z

we honour the first custodians of this land
their spirit moving through earth and sky and water
country is breath and memory intertwined
stories sung in wind through rock and leaf
each partnership a promise of respect and care
when we listen deeply we learn to walk together
building safe spaces where culture leads the way

HEATHER ANNE GORDON

A catalogue record for this book is available from the National Library of Australia

978-1-7635635-2-0
Title: Outback Lily episodes from a to z
Author: © Heather Anne Gordon 2018 - 2025

Acknowledgements:

We acknowledge and respect the deep spiritual connection and the relationship that First Nations people have to Country. Country takes in everything within the landscape – landforms, waters, air, trees, rocks, plants, animals, foods, medicines, minerals, stories and special places. Connections to Country include cultural practices, knowledge, songs, stories and art, as well as all people: past, present and future.

Kokatha, Barngarla, Kuyani, Adnyamathanha Country:
Andamooka area
Ngadjuri, Peramangk, Kaurna Country:
Barossa Valley region
South Australia

Internal design by Karen Engel
Cover art by Heather Anne Gordon

Dedicated to feminists everywhere: your courage, actions, voices, and stories ignite hope while working towards genuine equality and equity. The personal is political.

Centred in Choice
'Sharing Australian voices, stories, strategies and skills with the world.'
ABN 17 601 690 975 https://centredinchoice.com
PO Box 448 Alice Springs Northern Territory 0871 Australia

Outback Lily (the fictional character) is named after the dramatic lily flower that blooms in the arid zone after soaking rain. Just like the ephemeral yet resilient flower, stories from this collection of verses represent change, flourishing in the most unexpected places.

Outback Lily (the flower) is more commonly known as the Andamooka Lily. It is also known as the Darling Lily and Stink Lily. Stink Lily because it has strongly scented flowers which emit an unpleasant fragrance in the evenings.

Lily was asked, sarcastically,

'What planet do you live on?'

Lily answered, genuinely,

'I don't know. I'm an outlier. An outsider.'

In the outback of Australia, things happen.

Is Lily a participant, or an observer?

Witness, or …?

Embark on some adventures with Outback Lily as she travels the arid zone of South Australia in her sturdy camper van. Along the way, Outback Lily gathers campfire tales of adventure, boundary-breaking, courage, and defiance. Each episode, one from each letter of the alphabet, unveils stories already known to women, reframing them to challenge norms, embrace risks, and celebrate living unapologetically. With the occasional plot twist that can turn heartache, rejection, and pain into a catalyst for a more authentic life, these stories remind us that revenge is best served unexpectedly.

Warning! These outback narratives just might challenge your perspectives and awaken your inner risk-taker.

Written in random alphabetical order. Not intended to be read in alphabetical order. Outback Lily is unconventional and does not follow poetry conventions.

allegedly

in the heart of the arid outback lies Matrix Ridge
a town where despair and sorrows bridge
the welcome sign   a red mosaic heart aglow
dominates the landscape where harsh winds blow
dusty roads   wind through sparse vegetation
mullock heaps hug the horizon   a desolate creation
the scorching sun beats down   relentless   severe
casting long shadows   whispering secrets unclear

Lily returns to her old town its spirit long since gone
empty shop windows stare uselessly at faces tight and drawn
with Buddy the dog Lily strolls the dusty streets
at dusk she parks her camper van   seeking relief from the heat
running water   one shower stall one sink one flickering bulb
feeling emptiness beyond belief
Lily returns   some hope in her heart to win the love
of townsfolk   to make a fresh start   her childhood here
marred by trauma and disdain can good deeds heal the pain

Lily and Buddy walk through the town in the early morn
met with suspicious glances   hearts bitter and worn
undeterred   Lily begins her mission of grace
determined to bring smiles   to each hardened face
helping the elderly with odd jobs and errands
both her kindness and joy they are determined to withstand
Lily continues organizing clean-ups to beautify the town
hoping a cleaner place might turn frowns around

supporting local businesses with unwavering zeal
promoting them online to boost their appeal
tutoring children with patience and care
providing a safe space for them to learn and share
charity events Lily plans with tireless might
raising funds for causes   making things right
but her efforts are met with suspicion and scorn
the townspeople's hearts are hardened   stubborn

Buddy is a beacon for Lily in this bleak land
love unconditional always at hand
but when Buddy falls into a mine shaft deep
the townspeople turn away   leaving Lily to weep

Lily's heart hardens   this ultimately cruel act
finally realizing her efforts have no impact
Lily decides to expose the town's hidden lies
writing her story so the truth can rise
with words as her weapons she writes all night
hoping to bring darkness into the light   with her tale of Buddy
at least she tried   in a world so unhappy
where justice hides deeper than a mine shaft
it is Lily who feels shafted

in Matrix Ridge where secrets and lies intertwine
Lily pens a tale of shadows sinister and serpentine
chapters released online   truth stored in the cloud
yet there is silence   nothing from the crowd

no reaction no change in sight   the bitterness sustained
by the lonely dark of night   Lily's frustration
turns to burning rage
she determines to set fires   to make the town engage
so in the early hours   before the moon sleeps
she silently observes the first blaze as it steadily creeps
the C F S struggles to contain the fiery parade
even with help from the next town's fire brigade

each night a new fire closer to the heart

the town's panic grows as the flames start

the hot north winds gust spreading the blaze

shade cloth and pvc tanks consumed in the haze

Lily observes from a distance but not too far

her heart a mix of sorrow and scar

the flames a metaphor for her own release

burning away the past   finding inner peace

Matrix Ridge is ruined   reduced to ash

the townspeople claim victimhood

in a flash   they raise money online   desperate

ignorant of the bitterness   unaware of the culprit

Lily drives away without looking back

carrying lessons learned   now on a new track

Lily vows to never be trapped again

finding her strength in fire and her courage within

in the back of Lily's camper van

the innocent-looking pliers   so sly   the key to the plan

cause sparks and short circuits   fires they can command

they nudge other tools   in Lily's home maintenance kit

ready for malice   they readily admit

© Heather Anne Gordon
January 2022

bravely

early life

boldly   bravely   brazenly

beautiful Lily

beneath boundless skies

battles burdens

best friends beside

brilliantly bright

    becoming

beyond boundaries

    blossoming

mid-life

bravely battling   boldly bright

brazen Lily   burning light

beneath boundless skies   she fights

breaking barriers   breaching heights

best friends beside   they never belittle

bouncing back   un-breakable

bottled burdens   now belied

beautiful Lily   empowered stride

battled stalking   belittlement too

now brazenly bold   breaking through

resilient spirit   strong and true

becoming brilliant   blooming anew

bravely   bumbling and stumbling
breaking old barriers   brave Lily
un-bottled burdens and branded by battles
blocked but never bowed
bowling through bloody days
blanking out black days
burrowing deep with borrowed strength
busily becoming   blossoming

brumby wild because of the blurred lines

feeling
burdened but bright   bowed but un-broken
blunt but brilliant   boxed in but banked on
often bamboozled   aiming for betterment

buffoons
blundering but back peddling
blaming and backstabbing
bee-like   buzzing
brainless blowflies

bumbling bewildered bureaucrats

being blamed
blind-sided but not buckled
but bucked and fucked by billions of voices
backroom battles
battle-scarred but Brisbane bound
biding time bravely

the barmaid
better   but still bawling
and brawling   barstools sprawling
temper boiling   bad balls   spoiling
blunt instrument calling

botched job
blundered and bundled
barina car   a backhoe   burying those balls
a bold ballerina move
burnt   her body battered   brittle
but un-broken   not bottlo bound
not bitter   not burdened

currently

borrowed blue bicycle

breezily bright

best friends beside

balanced and big hearted

so brilliant Lily

© Heather Anne Gordon
May 2025

consequently

Lily listened
as her friend confided her story
a tale   as old as time
filled with pain   and worry
about sexual assault and mental health
a heavy weight to bear
blame the woman   protect the perpetrator
it is so unfair

I was raped at work   she blurted bravely
sharing her story   sought counselling
told just a few friends   feeling angry
a well-meaning friend reported it   to H R
without asking   the workplace took action
demanded   a meeting

confronted my rapist in front of a panel
feeling so small   he got to ask me questions
sneering through it all   a friend asked
are you sure you remember it right
I spiralled in shame   lost   afraid
day and night

and then they ruled
in his favour   a crushing blow
he got a restraining order
he is free to come and go   consequently
I had to find a new job   haunted by fear
he still stalks my nightmares   always near

I found
some of his other victims   none had taken action
none wanted to discuss it   no criminal traction
because they already knew   what I had learned
no one ever believes
the women   our cries are unheard

the world
is wired   to shut us up
silence our voice   nothing changes
is there a choice
there is a price to pay
for speaking out   it is true
for anyone
who cannot share their story   this one is for you

do we

band together   take him out

the criminal justice system

doesn't care   there is no doubt

is that our choice   to make things right

is speaking out

the only way   to continue the fight

blame the woman   protect the perpetrator

it is the same   using rape

and assault   to intimidate   it is a cruel game

the perpetrator is applauded   promoted to high office

sometimes even the highest   a twisted orifice

the presumption of innocence

twisted and warped   to work in his favour

leaving victims scorched

we must speak up

about this   never stop the fight

even men of good will   need to see the light

confronted with how much   men benefit

from this terror   explicit porn

sexually violent acts   practiced together

their brutality enabled

by those   who refuse to believe

victim survivors   left to grieve

blame the woman   protect the perpetrator
it is the norm   we do speak up   we do create
a word storm
Outback Lily listened   calm
non-judgemental   with strength and resolve
her attitude   unsentimental

how to empower
the silenced   let their voices be heard
is it enough   to stand together
changing the world   word by word

raising awareness
about signs   of relationship strife
educating   about healthy relationships
changing lives   preventing abuse
encouraging victims to seek   help
when they need it   and being strong
when they are feeling weak

providing
support services   hotlines   and shelters too
counselling   legal aid   helping them start anew
escaping
abusive situations   rebuilding their lives
in this way   support for victims thrives

strengthening

laws to protect   and hold accountable

restraining orders   penalties

make justice attainable

training law enforcement   to handle with care

family violence cases   ensuring they are fair

encouraging

involvement from community allies

friends   family   neighbours

organisations that rise   together

their support   creating a strong network

helping those affected   doing vital work

empowering victims with

advocacy and tools   financial independence

education   changing rules

job training   access   control of their fate

providing resources   opening that gate

addressing norms

and attitudes

that perpetuate   family violence

a long-term change

to create   promoting equality   respect

non-violence the key   in society's fabric

a new norm we see

remember

we all play a role in this fight

ending family violence

making it right   working together

creating support and care

a safer environment for everyone to share

Lily sharpens the blades

in her home maintenance kit

her mind incisive

shrewd   decisive   it is time

to make the hit

sick of talking sick of men ignoring

Lily knows

this night will not be boring

© Heather Anne Gordon
January 2024

deliberately

voting deliberately: voices of the outback

in the outback's vast expanse
Lily stands   an outlier   an outsider
in a land where democracy's flame
burns bright

compulsory voting   a deed of civic pride
where every voice is heard   every citizen has a say

in the heart of Australia
we gather   sausages grilling
a celebration of rights   a democratic feast

young and old
we cast our votes   deliberately
with purpose   shaping the future of our land
the A E C   a guiding hand
fair and transparent
ensuring every vote counts
every voice is valued

voting deliberately: voices of the outback

inclusion is our strength
from pre-poll to postal
telephone ballots and all
a system built on trust

yet   some refrain   a blank ballot
a silent claim
but democracy persists   strong and true
Australia   a beacon
compulsory voting our pride
a century of high turnout
a testament to our resolve

in the outback's quiet
Lily's voice joins the chorus
a participant   and an observer
in the song and dance of democracy

© Heather Anne Gordon
January 2025

in Australia's vast expanse
where democracy's flame burns bright
compulsory voting stands
a deed of civic pride
every eligible adult
must cast their vote deliberately
to exercise their democratic right
no excuse   no apathy

the A E C ensures transparency
a guiding hand   fair and clear
from pre-poll to postal
telephone ballots for all to hear
democracy sausages
a celebration of achievement
a festive treat   a voter's delight
where everyone has the legal right

apathy is the enemy of democracy
a silent threat   a creeping blight
while U S politics might seem exciting
Australia's 90% turnout is our guiding light
getting your name ticked off the roll
ensures eligible citizens have input
a system built on trust and pride
where every vote counts   every voice is valued

across Australia   we gather
sausages grilling   a celebration of rights
a democratic feast   a civic duty fulfilling
by engaging in voting
knowledge grows   understanding issues
and which issues the candidates oppose

with compulsory participation
minds expand   political awareness   across the land
compelled to enrol   yet some refrain
a blank or marred ballot   their silent claim

but democracy persists
strong and true   Australia   a leader
compulsory voting our pride
a century of high turnout
a testament to our resolve
deliberate voting   keeps the centre strong

moderates thrive   extremes rarely belong
not just partisans   casting their say
Australia's balance
leads the way   deliberate voting
keeps balance clear

moderates' voices   we hold dear
polarisation quelled   grievances stall
Australia resists   the populist call
deliberate voting   strong institutions stand

bolstering confidence   across the land
despite some disaffection
trust holds sway   with the A E C
guiding the democratic way
Australia's fair   and steady hand

democracy   and trust command
with Saturday voting
and support so wide
inclusive voting   our nation's pride
deliberate voting   strong and true

few controversies   support comes through

enforced consistently   citizens comply

Australia's example   standards held high

Australia

cannot be complacent

it is true   low turnout in remote areas

a challenge to view   Australia's voting system

it is upheld   the most voter-friendly

in the world   deliberate voting

ensures the way   accessibility

smooths the way   each election day

Australia's ease   a model so rare

contrasts with struggles   seen elsewhere

deliberate voting   Aussie pride

a century's norm   the world's eyes wide

casual familiarity   breeds apathy

staying vigilant   is democracy's key

© Heather Anne Gordon
January 2025

in Australia   voting's a compulsory deed
democracy in action   it is quite agreed
sticks and carrots   guide the way
so every eligible citizen has a say

contrast   the U S A   and the U K
their voter turnout   is not the same way
here in Australia   we all must vote
with sausages grilling   take note!

young hearts   chase the thrill   of U S debates
while Aussie politics fades   a distant hum
lost in the apathy of disengaged youth
Aboriginal voices   rose for the Referendum
but dirty media and lying politicians
shattered trust   leaving hope in the dust

yet the A E C persists
an independent beacon of trust
maintaining the roll
conducting elections   fair   transparent
and free from political shadows   standing tall

A E C's mobile booths
on the go   pre-poll   postal
or at the embassy you can go
telephone ballots
for those with low vision
inclusive voting   every single election

democracy barbeque   a voter's delight
where everyone   over eighteen
has the legal right   it is more than duty
it is a right to civic acclaim
Australia's elections   a democratic flame

every citizen   their voice they raise
in Australia's elections   we all have our say
deliberate voting   a right so true
each person's choice   a value imbued

whether first-time voter
or seasoned pro
the importance of voting   we should all know
an inclusive system   for all to see
a democratic nation   proud to be

a celebration of rights   so grand and fair
united in voting   with pride to spare
democracy sausages   a festive treat
voting is like having a barbeque
for everyone in the street

by engaging in voting   knowledge grows
understanding issues   which issues candidates oppose
with compulsory participation   minds expand
political awareness   across the land
compelled to attend   yet some refrain
a blank or marred ballot   their silent claim
apathetic folks   in line they float
numbering boxes   casting a "donkey vote"

in the early twentieth century's rise
Australia's innovation   took the prize
with secret ballots   for voting fair
electoral systems   beyond compare.

democracy   with an Aussie flair
preferential voting   everywhere
non-partisan   clear   and true
pioneers   in democracy's queue

Australia   stands alone   so bold
compulsory voting   a story told
Britain   Canada   the States   and Kiwis
voluntary systems   while Australia's
is compulsory

unlike others   Australia stands firm
compulsory voting   we affirm
enforced by courts   upheld with grace
sanctions   ensure compliance   in place

compulsory voting   a century strong
high voter turnout   show we belong
ninety percent   the standard's set
Australia's democracy   the best bet

Australia's turnout   thirty percent higher
than those nations   with voluntary vote fire
voluntary systems   they cannot compete
our compulsory voting   a turnout feat

the public backs it   strong and true
half a century's polls   they prove it too
support stays steady   around seventy percent
compulsory voting   with firm consent

deliberately voting   keeps the centre strong
moderates thrive   extremes rarely belong
not just partisans   casting their say
Australia's balance   leads the way.

deliberately voting   keeps balance clear
moderates' voices   we hold dear
polarisation quelled   grievances stall
Australia resists   the populist call

deliberately voting   strong institutions stand
bolstering confidence   across the land
despite some disaffection   trust holds sway
with the A E C guiding the democratic way

Australia's fair and steady A E C hand
democracy   and trust command
with Saturday voting and support so wide
inclusive voting   our nation's pride

deliberately voting   strong and true
few controversies   support comes through
enforced consistently   citizens comply
Australia's example   standards held high

Australia   cannot be complacent
it is true   low turnout in remote areas
a challenge to view   Australia's voting system
it is upheld   the most voter-friendly
in the world

deliberately voting   ensures the way
accessibility   smooths the way
each election day   Australia's ease
a model so rare   contrasts with struggles
seen elsewhere
deliberately voting   Aussie pride
a century's norm   world's eyes wide
casual familiarity   breeds apathy
staying vigilant is Democracy's key

© Heather Anne Gordon
January 2025

Democracy sausages (meat or vegan) for everyone!
Democracy sausages (optional)
Democracy voting (compulsory)

voting deliberately: democracy warning

Australia's voting system   quite unique
with preferences to tweak
in the House   each candidate you note
while in the Senate   at least six to vote

two main parties   in the fray
A L P or L N P   you must weigh
even if neither's in your heart's alignment
one of these two will lead the government.

Currently   Albanese of the A L P
stands in the centre's light
Dutton is far right
in the Liberal National Party Coalition's might
being centrist isn't extreme
despite what some may say and scheme

Not all L N P side with Trump that's clear
Albanese's centre is calm and near
friends and followers may split
choose the middle   avoid the on-the-right
cesspit

Liberal ties to Trump are strong
Morrison's visit for the New Year's song
Rhinehart's big cheer at Trump's big night
Vote left   or centrist   to be all right

before Trump's second term stirred the land
Rhinehart said to Watch Learn and Stand
Dutton follows Trump's policies bold
shrinks government   targets E O
says there are only two genders
walked out on the Apology
to the Stolen Generations

Rhinehart's bond with the Coalition is tight
sees herself in Musk's own light
with Dutton as P M in her sight
her power grows an ambitious flight

Trump's extreme neoliberal guise
corporate rules axed   no disguise
taxes for the rich deeply slashed
a realm once unthinkable now trashed

Trump is ticking off Project Twenty Twenty-five's list
Heritage Foundation's opaque twist
far-right agenda not hidden but planned
shaping the future with a heavy hand

C E Os watch upheavals unfold
goal posts shift   ambitions bold
self-interest reigns   society's bane
Earth and people   face the strain

Rhinehart's wish is crystal clear
low taxes   wages kept austere
minimal rules for work and Earth
regulations light   fascism's rebirth

low corporate tax billionaires' delight
wages low   rules loose on site
no carbon tax   pollution controls thin
minimal regs for maximum win

Dutton's silent on the billionaire's feast
but he will shout about crime   defence increased
immigration   anti-woke   cost of living
anti-Semitism too   his focus unforgiving

Dutton's choice   a wand in hand
Reinhart's list would swiftly stand
Ignoring ethical points in a trice
Reinhart's joy   no compromise

before U S green tape there were rivers ablaze
Cuyahoga's fire with oil's harsh gaze
junked cars leaking   streams defiled
laws absent   pollution wild

since 1970 when Nixon took the stage
environmental laws to gauge
awareness surged concerns   so real
regulations set   the deal sealed

environmental laws once stood tall
a bipartisan cause uniting all
transcending politics   both sides agreed
protection for nature   a shared creed

is Dutton seeking to follow Trump's ride?
an opportunist   with ambitions wide?
harnessing   the far-right's might
to catapult himself to The Lodge's light

can we be sure he'll drop Trump's guise?
return to the Coalition's old ties?
or will he charge on with the far-right's spree?
egged on by Rhinehart, Murdoch and actions we see?

we cannot be sure that Rhinehart's dismayed
by Trump's actions so extreme and frayed
inspiration   might she take in stride
emulate his ways   and not just abide

cost of living   immigration is to blame
we must refute   the housing crisis
needs a broader pursuit
growth and recession   both intertwined
an adult talk needed with open minds

yet Albanese's term   scandals and rorts none
avoidable crises   none in view
China relations being mended and strong
it is a steady path that Albo leads the cabinet along

with a touch of fiscal flair
Treasurer Chalmers made us all aware
from fourteenth to top three
a feat the world could see
I M F applause for balanced fiscal laws
Labor's careful hand should bring confidence
to the land

protected in Australia from excesses stark
by leadership structure a guiding mark
no executive orders to sway the tide
a stable path where we can bide
under Dutton worse could unfold
in a volatile world with stories told
of Trump's pressure   Executive Orders
tariffs in play   friends and foes
might sway our way

any worse   might bring a Musk-like reign
Government shutdowns   freedom's strain
far-right takeover   Orwellian might
democracy subverted   will we wake in fright?

Fascism feeds on fear's cruel game
brave people know they might be named
rule of law crumbles   threat draws near
targets are those who hold courage dear

they face unknown dangers as fears collide
yet stand firm with hearts open wide
though peril's shadow looms in view
they act with honour knowing it is true

Australia stands alone   no Bill of Rights in sight
a developed nation yet lacking this basic right
it is time we recognise   and take a stand
for rights protected across our land

raising this topic might bring yawns
cynicism is cool until your rights are gone
extremists trample   freedoms shake
a wake-up call for action's sake

the absence of a Bill of Rights
a vital need   complacency will not help us lead
"She'll be right" is no longer wise
proactive steps ensure our lives

if the Coalition's your usual vote
consider Labor   maybe a Teal   and take note
this time around a choice to make
an enormous difference it could create

those who seek insurance shielded and wise
know the value of securing their ties
understanding the need for a safety net
hoping they grasp the message clearly set

for healthier elections   truth   we must guard
the Australia Institute's call is not too hard
no rules to stop lies   except S A's way
reforming the system   truth should hold sway

GetUp! Fights for reform to unfold
curbing dark money   a story told
transparency in politics their drive
to ensure democracy can truly thrive

apply healthy scepticism   agnostic
and clear   to election claims
from every side you hear
scrutinize each photo   video   and speech
for ayy-eye deepfakes could be within reach

in election's midst   truth must be our guide
with a sceptical eye   let's set aside pride
guard against the far-right's tightening grip
choose wisely   for Democracy's ship

Vote. Deliberately.

© Heather Anne Gordon
January 2025

verse 1

In the heart of the outback, where the red dust flies,

We gather 'round the polling place, under southern skies.

With a sausage sizzle and a smile so wide,

We cast our votes, with Aussie pride.

chorus

Oh, we vote in Australia, it is our civic right

From the cities to the bush, we stand and fight.

For democracy and freedom, we all unite,

In the land down under, we vote with might.

verse 2

From the coast to the desert, every voice is heard,

With the A E C guiding, fair and undeterred.

No excuse for apathy, we all take a stand,

To shape our future, in this great southern land.

chorus

Oh, we vote in Australia, it is our civic right,

From the cities to the bush, we stand and fight.

For democracy and freedom, we all unite,

In the land down under, we vote with might.

verse 3

Deliberate and informed, we make our choice,

Finding out about policies, not just slogans' noise.

With a pen in hand, we mark the ballot true,

Every vote counts, it is up to me and you.

chorus

Oh, we vote in Australia, it is our civic right,

From the cities to the bush, we stand and fight.

For democracy and freedom, we all unite,

In the land down under, we vote with might.

verse 4

The young and the old, we all play our part,

With a sense of duty, and a hopeful heart.

Ninety percent turnout, we lead the way,

In Australia, on election day.

chorus

Oh, we vote in Australia, it is our civic right,

From the cities to the bush, we stand and fight.

For democracy and freedom, we all unite,

In the land down under, we vote with might.

verse 5

So let's celebrate, with a sausage in hand,

In this great democracy, across the land

For every vote cast, is a voice that's heard,

In the land down under, we spread the word.

chorus

Oh, we vote in Australia, it is our civic right,

From the cities to the bush, we stand and fight.

For democracy and freedom, we all unite,

In the land down under, we vote with might.

© Heather Anne Gordon
January 2025

exceptionally

Lily is travelling
setting her own trail
experimenting
with art and words
creating her own tale
many projects unfinished
always something new
Lily is impulsive
sometimes acting
without a clue

Lily is caring and kind
loves people   you see
but Lily's an outlier
and that's the key
an outlier's a person
unique in kind
outside the norm
different in mind

in statistics
an outlier sits outside
the spread
Lily's out of the norm
trying to stay ahead
some good abilities
yet deficiencies too
Lily struggles to belong
in her own view

Lily tries many things
wants to excel
although
in some skills
Lily does not do so well
emotionally sensitive
sometimes she is stuck
Lily is unique
and that is just her luck

unconventional background
childhood poverty
Lily's ideas are distinct
part of her innate   creativity
is the community judgemental?
what does Lily care?
Lily's resilient spirit
shines everywhere

reflective and observant
Lily knows her skills
leveraging what is easy
to climb those hills
communicating   relating
with a friendly tone
yet   burning those bridges
yet   trying not to be alone

with courage to act
Lily shows her truth
looking for allies
at the voting booth
Lily's embracing her rage
standing tall
no longer polite
Lily's breaking the wall

taking time to reflect
observing the world
understanding her strengths
letting them unfurl
knowing her struggles
finding a new way
achieving her goals
then trying again each day

risk is unacceptable
some ideas might fall
but allies are there
trusting overall
sparking connections
building a new crew
outlier Lily
always breaking through

from the outback landscape
to the city streets
Lily is on a journey
Lily will not accept defeat
being different is tough
it is true
but in Lily's uniqueness
dreams do break through

so   if you are an outlier
much like Lily
embrace your strengths
they make you free
communicate
relate   with warmth and grace
like outlier Lily   stay in the race

keep that courage
act with intent
show vulnerability
but never relent
Lily's journey
let it inspire
spark the strength in you
set your passion on fire

© Heather Anne Gordon
May 2023

flourishingly

staying motivated
it is a breeze for me
with ideas flowing like a lively sea
projects galore
always on the go
it is wrapping them up that is tricky   you know

short projects
they get done   they reach the end
it is the big ones that challenge and transcend
one novel published
three more on their way.
no magic wand
but here is what the writing gurus say

pick a topic you know
be it places or faces
from the freewheeling hell of life's many cases
is there a spark of interest
let curiosity steer
go deeper
explore
let your passion be clear

know why you are writing
let your passion ignite
it is the intrinsic reward that brings delight
beyond external praise
find joy in your art
writing from the heart
it is where you start

be clear on the scope
main characters and theme
key elements to cover   like a well-planned dream
this clarity helps
research   it will not be a mess
stay focused and calm
avoid any overwhelming stress

make time each day for your book
if you can
consistency is key
stick to the plan
realistic goals will keep you on track
dedication each day
no looking back

remember   a finished book
though not perfect and neat
is worth much more
than an unfinished feat
an imperfect story holds value and grace
while a perfect draft
left undone
has no place

writing with friends
and joining groups
is key
an editor can guide you   it is easy to see
consider Jena Jaensch   at Six Degrees
her expertise
will help your writing project
with ease

gather readers who deeply care
ready to engage and be fair
prepared to offer feedback kind
on every page that they find
their insights will shape your tale
with their constructive critique
your writing will prevail

sharing their thoughts
with each twist and turn
helping your passion
to ignite and burn
their voices guide
their wisdom shares
in the world of writing
find a publisher who really cares

embrace the writing challenge
be brave and strive
reach beyond your experience
your dreams come alive
step out of your comfort
let courage be your guide
into the unknown.
find strength on the other side

ignore those who disparage
those filled with disdain
your writing is for you
they have nothing to gain
stay true to your voice
let your passion resound
their negativity fades
when your purpose is found

shake off that feeling
you do not owe them a thing
write for yourself
let your true voice sing
your story   your journey
it is all on your terms
find joy in the process   let your passion affirm

you are writing for yourself
not just to impress
if they think they know you
they might be quite perplexed
your novels could surprise
showing a different side
embrace your unique voice
let your creativity guide

avoid
over explaining to the critics
they truly will not see
your writing is for you   let it simply be
share with those who vibe
with your creative stream
let the rest just fade   like a distant dream

ignore opinions
from those who do not create
focus on your craft
leave behind their hate
your passion and drive
make your work so cool
their judgments are nothing   they are the fool

to stay motivated
choose a topic you adore
stay curious and joyful
let your passions soar
set clear goals
write daily
do not stress about perfection
find joy in the process   let that be your direction

there is no need
to try and prove your worth
your talents and passions
have value on this earth
stay true to yourself
let your spirit be free
your unique light shines   that is all you need to be

© Heather Anne Gordon
January 2024

gracefully

#Let Her Speak

at fifteen
Grace faced a predator's cruel game
but her spirit burned bright
like an unyielding flame
he thought she would be silent
but Grace stood tall
her resilience
and justice
inspiring us all

at sixteen
Grace's courage shone bright
she reported Nicolaas Bester
seeking justice and light
convicted and imprisoned
he faced his due
Grace's strength
inspires
through and through

at twenty-two
Grace fought
for her voice
against a law
that silenced
her choice
while her abuser
spoke freely
she sought to reclaim
her right to tell her story
in her own name

sexual abuse
is not just physical pain
it is the calculated
manipulation
that leaves a stain
meticulous control
a predator's cruel art
but survivors like Grace
show the strength
of the heart

it is crucial

to discuss

and we must not ignore

abusers

prey

on those whose lives are worn

they exploit

the vulnerable

thinking they will win

but survivors like Grace

show the strength within

abusers

seek out

those who are alone

in unstable lives

where

seeds of fear

are sown

they prey

on the vulnerable

thinking they will win

but survivors like Grace

show the strength within

step one

is targeting

a victim they seek

finding the vulnerable

the isolated

the meek

in shadows

they lurk

with intentions so vile

preying on the lonely

with a pleasant smile

step two

is gaining trust

a rapport

they start to build

conning the victim

with false support

instilled

validation offered

but it is all a deceit

in this twisted game

the trap

is almost complete

step three
is filling a need
a gap they seek to find
in the victim's life
they weave a web
so intertwined
with false promises
they fill the void
with lies
a predator's deceit
disguised

step four
is grooming
to isolate and divide
driving wedges deep
where support used to reside
cutting off connections
leaving the victim alone
in the predator's grip
true colours are shown

step five
is insidious
gradual
in its guise
sexualization
creeps in
with subtle ties
introducing concepts
in conversations
they weave
exposing
to content
a trap
hard to perceive

step six
is control
a balance they maintain
causing pain
then relief
in a twisted chain
confusion
and guilt
the victim's mind
they sway
silencing their voice
keeping truth at bay

the abuser
crafts an image
powerful and grand
intimidating presence
with a heavy hand
in shadows they loom
with a fearsome guise
their power a façade
built on deceit and lies

guilt
weighs heavy
with threats
that subtly creep
in shadows
they whisper
promises
they keep
a mind ensnared
in a web of fear
indirect threats
making intentions clear

Grace
has changed laws
brought
understanding
to light
given strength
and hope
turning wrongs into right
a beacon for survivors
her courage shines through
inspiring others
with the hope
that they too can renew

at twenty-six
Grace stood tall
in the spotlight's glow
Australian of the Year
her courage we now know
her fight for justice
her voice ringing clear
inspiring a nation
with hope and cheer

at the twenty twenty-two Awards

Grace's side-eye was bold

Prime Minister Morrison

a story unfolds

the media in a frenzy

but Grace's message

was clear

Grace's courage

and strength

we should all hold dear

Grace

spoke out

her voice strong and clear

criticizing Morrison

the government's fear

Grace called out the failures

the plans left behind

for family and domestic violence

a better path to find

Grace

aghast at Morrison's first stance

when Brittany spoke out

the significance

Grace's voice

for justice

a call to be heard

Grace stood

with strength

her message undeterred

Morrison

spoke with his wife

seeking insight

Jenny urged him to think

as a father

with daughters in sight

reflecting

on Brittany's pain

a call to be fair

a reminder

of empathy

for those who care

Grace

spoke with passion

on the Press Club's stage

saying

conscience is not just from a parent's gauge

having children

does not guarantee what's right

our morals should guide us

day and night

Grace Tame in twenty twenty-five

wearing block letters of black and red

her t-shirt brought some questions

and the media led

offended by her message

time for a reality check

her courage

voice

and vision

earn our respect

Grace Tame

a beacon

of strength and cheer

attended the 2025 Awards

her message clear

at The Lodge in Canberra

Grace stood with pride

a survivor

an advocate

with courage as her guide

Grace wore a t-shirt reading plainly

FUCK

MURDOCH

the media

snapped Grace

next to Albanese's side

stories penned quickly

her presence amplified

a picture worth thousands

her strength standing tall

Grace's journey

and voice

should inspire us all

social platforms
buzzed
with debates all around
Grace's protest
sparking
discussions profound
was it the right time and place
opinions collide
but Grace's courage
and message
cannot be denied

Albanese
weighed in
calling Grace's actions
"wrong"
saying Grace took focus
from those brave and strong
but Grace's message echoed
amidst the debate
a reminder of truth
in matters of state

when it suits
the government's goal
individuals shine
like Grace
upheld for change to align
a poster child
for justice
her truth on display
Grace's message
and courage
are here to stay

Grace's power
and courage
bring light to the night
Grace's story of trauma
ignites others' fight
opening up
about pain
Grace helps others heal
Grace's strength
and her voice
a resilient appeal

with fearless voice

and unwavering drive

Grace protests

and ruptures

keeping hopes alive

Grace was chosen

Australian of the Year

twenty twenty-one

for battles she fought

and the victories won

in a t-shirt brave

her personal protest stood

a scar from childhood

Murdoch's stories never could

exploit her trauma

for profit they chase

Grace's resilience

in the midst of their

disgrace

it is not just

public protests

but the core beliefs inside

media and government rattled

with truths they cannot abide

the beliefs strong in Grace's voice

causing ripples wide

a call for justice

no longer to be

denied

criticizing

Grace's shirt

it is shaky ground they tread

beholden to Murdoch's circus

where loyalty is fed

rarely rewarded

yet shameless

they remain

in the media's grip

their actions seem so

vain

our Prime Minister's
response
a letdown in the fray
a chance
to show backbone
slipping away
in these times
strength
is what we need
yet disappointment
is all we see
agreed

ordinary Aussies
weary
of the media's reign
monopoly unchecked
causing
much disdain
yearning for truth
with scrutiny so rare
hoping
for a future
where fairness
is in the air

Grace's protest
embraced
by many with hearts
she was demonstrating
in that shirt
her message clear
Grace wore
what we are feeling
her courage
sparked a unity
a message far and wide
saying what needs saying
no longer brushed aside

Grace
took a stand
her platform loud and bright
a voice for many
who stay hidden from the fight
what we admire most
her courage so profound
in her strength
our collective voice
has found

Grace

wore a message

sparked conversation anew

that was the essence

with words so true

tell me

which part

holds disrespect's mark

in her boldness

she simply

lit a spark

at thirty
Grace wrote thirty rules for life
you can find them on your device
no one says it better than Grace

hopefully

through the shadows
cast by power's grip
we rise
with strength of spirit
and hope
in our eyes
in every heart
a story
of courage untold
feminist energy
fierce and bold

in a world
where justice fights
a backward tide
our dreams
of progress
they cannot hide
for every step back
we rise anew
feminist energy
with hope
bold and true

backwards
we go
on rights
and the earth
ignoring diversity
women
migrants' worth
yet
in the face of regress
hope takes flight
feminist energy
shining through the night

in shadows
cast by tech bros might
dreams of other planets
will not make our wrongs right
while masculine forces they decree
feminist energy
rises with hope
fierce and free

through the media's lens
we see power's cruel might
masculine forces
casting shadows in the night
yet hope endures
in whispers and cries
feminist energy
rising
breaking ties

masculine forces
drive conflict's cruel game
in Ukraine and Gaza
it fuels the flame
yet hope persists
in hearts that defy
feminist energy
rising
reaching the sky

in Sudan and Darfur
shadows of wars
masculine forces
leave wounds and scars
yet hope endures
in whispers and cries
feminist energy
rising
breaking ties

in Afghanistan
voices silenced
dreams confined
masculine forces
erase
leave hope behind
yet in the shadows
whispers of light
feminist energy
ready to ignite

in twenty twenty-four
the heat broke through
one point five degrees celsius
a warning we knew
yet hope survives
in hearts that fight,
feminist energy
shining so bright

while billionaires
dream
of Mars' faraway lands
earth's warnings
are clearly in our hands
bushfires
floods
cyclones
droughts in sight
feminist energy
striving
to make it right

masculine forces
a failing creed
for all genders
they plant a divisive seed
patriarchy
colonialism
racism in its wake
feminist energy
the change
we must make

feminist leadership
a guiding light
in a world that spirals
it shines so bright
with empathy
it shows the way
feminist energy
leading us to a better day

a feminist call
a beacon so clear
start at home
at work
bring change near
in communities
justice and equity unfurled
feminist energy
shaping
a sustainable world

each day we rise
with purpose clear
feminist principles
guiding us here
to be the change we wish to see
feminist energy
setting our spirits free

a world of justice

free from oligarchy's reign

where poverty

and oppression

feel no gain

transformative

feminist leaders in sight

feminist energy

guiding us

unite

leaders who share

not dominate or bind

building power within

hearts and minds

together we rise

united and strong

feminist energy

so we all belong

© Heather Anne Gordon
January 2025

ideally

art one oh one

art is a fortress
walled with gates so high
purposefully
hoarded by those
draped in gold

for the wealthy
inspiration applies
while the voiceless
watch their dreams
grow cold

creativity is a luxury denied
too many
crushed
by life's relentless grind

a system
built on falsehoods
lies
and pride

where few
can chase
their passions
free their minds

rage for a world
where art
is for
the masses

where every voice
and vision
boldly clashes

in hues
and forms
in dances
wild and free

art holds a mirror
to society's face
it speaks of justice
cries
for liberty

art transforms
the heart
and stirs us
to embrace

visuals
performance
installations bold

their power
is in truths
they dare to show

through brush and stage
their stories
behold

unveil the depths
of human joy
and woe

yet censorship's
cold hand
can stifle
the voice

and commerce
seeks
to tame
the artist's soul

these obstacles
though daunting
will not destroy

the fire within
that drives
to make us whole

for art
undaunted
thrives

through storm
and strife
a beacon

of our shared
unyielding
life

in frames of colour
shapes
and light confined
visual art
reveals
our social thread

it mirrors norms
our values
intertwined
and tells the tales
of times
we have lived and led

art binds us
to our culture
our roots
profound
its brushstrokes
speak
of ancient tales
and lore

in modern hues
new narratives
are found
reflecting shifts
and changes
at our core

through art
we see
the structures
of our lives
our institutions
power
and belief

it fosters
bonds
where emotion
thrives
and soothes
the heart
in joy
in pain
in grief

thus
art becomes
a bridge
from past to now
a guide to where
society can grow

in art's bold stroke
a truth
profound
is found
a call
for justice
echoed loud
and clear

through learnings
rich
where voices
once
were bound
new worlds
emerge
each one
devoid of fear

critical eyes
on power
structures gaze
reflexive minds
unravel
hidden threads

injustice's guise
in art's light
decays
a vision
bright
where equity
spreads

bear witness
then
to systems
old and frail
to biases
that mar
our shared
embrace

envision
realms
where fairness
will prevail
discrimination
gone
without a trace

arts-based
research
a beacon
in the night
guides us
towards
a future
just and bright

in strokes
notes
in words that
fiercely flow
art wields
the power
to ignite
our souls

it challenges
the status quo
we know
and casts
a light
where shadows
hide the trolls

through paint and song
through dance
and vivid play
art speaks
of justice
liberty
and peace

it amplifies
the voices
kept at bay
and strives
for love
and equity's
increase

art

breaks the chains

of silence

fear

and might

empowering

the voiceless

to unite

in its embrace

we find

the strength

to fight

for brighter days

and dreams

that take their flight

art

stands as beacon

guide

and heart's refrain

a powerful force

for change

in joy

and pain

© Heather Anne Gordon
July 2024

judgementally

nineteen eighty-four

"That's sexual harassment," the young woman said.
"Oooh, I'd love some sexual harassment," he goaded.
She knew a complaint would be in vain.
Management laughed
about the recent Equal Opportunity Act's refrain.

twenty eighteen

Lily sat around the campfire
feeling the night grow cold
as the women shared stories
of adventures long and bold
each word sparked a dream
in the flicker of the flame
Lily's heart dances with the tales
never to be the same

in the freedom of the outback
voices flew afar
women spoke their minds
beneath a sky full of stars
sharing tales and dreams
no bounds   no bars
in the heart of the bush
revealing their scars

their topics contentious
issues deeply held
in their careers   at times
their voices quelled
yet under the star their stories swelled
in unity   their truths   and fears
compelled

to blame women for silence
is to ignore their plight
their careers hanging by threads
in the darkness of night
from factory floors to executive doors   the trials they face
it is time we stood together
to ensure a safer place

the psychology is clear
the impact profound
humiliation and fear
in silence they are bound
if they dare speak out
careers on the line
labelled as "too sensitive"
their strength undermined

some women fend him off
but if they make a scene
the media tears them apart
cruel and mean
oh   it is just testosterone
they say with a scoff
ignoring the courage
it took to send him off

blaming women for his deeds
a cruel twist of fate
cognitive dissonance fuels
the unjust hate
the men knew   yet stayed silent
avoiding the fray
it is time to challenge the silence
and not look away

it is not women's duty
to police men's wrongs
in a world that subjugates
we have had to be strong
surviving on resilience
we navigate each day
in hopes for a world
where equality holds sway

some reasons victims struggle
to voice their pain
there is the shame for not fighting
fear of threats that constrain
authorities failing
victims' cries left unheard
injustice persists
their stories deferred

before you launch a witch hunt
take a moment to see
the pain and the struggle
the silent plea
victims of assault
their voices must be heard
in a world that often silences
let us amplify their word

women navigate a world
harsh and unkind
facing sexism   disempowerment
dreams confined
if anyone knows the struggles
of reality's strain
it is the women who have endured
time and again

women are not taking over
just asking for their due
a world where their potential shines
abuse bid adieu
free from harassment
and systemic chains
a better world for all
where fairness reigns

the jokes once dismissed
now seen in a new light
insults that festered
hidden from sight
realization dawns
as confidence repairs
a step towards respect
in a world that cares

too many women
who have bravely spoken out
faced career setbacks
their futures in doubt
sexualized and insulted
in workplaces and beyond
their strength and resilience
we must respond

though men often perpetrate
some women stand by
egging on the behaviour
or watching with a sigh
blaming the victims
in a twisted display
ignoring the pain
and the price women must pay

across the land
respect must be our aim
recall how Julia Gillard
faced unjust blame
some treated her poorly
their actions unfair
we need to do better
show respect and care

no matter the politics

respect should be the norm

sexist   degrading words

a disgraceful storm

our female Prime Minister faced it

a shameful display

we must change our attitudes

and pave a better way

misogyny's grip

by all genders displayed

placards held high

with insults arrayed

on Parliament's lawns

the hurtful words flew

a reminder of the work

we still have to do

patriarchal norms

deeply ingrained in our way

Australia must rise

towards a brighter day

a future that is respectful

intelligent and true

inclusive for all

where equality blooms anew

a victim's voice matters
no matter when it is heard
to doubt their courage
is truly absurd
to think they only seek money
is callous and blind
compassion and understanding
we must find

to think these are claims for fame
is to ignore the pain
why would anyone seek attention
through such disdain
abuse and humiliation
no gain in a man's game
their voices deserve belief
not doubt or shame

why speak up now
after decades have passed
the pain and the trauma
they still feel harassed
used for their gender
the memories remain
their voices now rise
to ease the ingrained pain

if you can brush off hurt
that is strength of your own
but do not tell others
to just let it alone
not all wounds are the same
nor the healing pace
respect each woman's journey
and give them their space

the "old boys' club" thrives
but now is the time
for women to rise
against the bullies' crime
enough is enough
the voices declare
no more tolerance
for behaviour unfair

the fact it was done then
does not make it right
it was covered up
kept out of sight
acceptable it was not
hidden by lies
now truth emerges
no more disguise

women should be safe

no fear   no flight

from harassment's shadow

to a future bright

in judgment's absence

let respect ignite

a workplace fair

where all can unite

© Heather Anne Gordon
October 2023

kaleidoscopically

Lily   at various times
gave career advice   with flair
in project work
she had found her own strengths   to be fair
embracing chaos   she would plan with might
helping others find their creative core
their own bright light

within the storm of dreams
and doubt
seeking purpose
a job that stands out
platitudes afloat   clouds of cliché
find your way in this chaos
play

mazes of hopes
and dreams
we weave
following passion   told to believe
in chaos   you will find your light
a spark that turns dark to bright

in the heart of chaos
dreams take wing
can you even do anything
yes   let freedom sing
unleash strength   inner might
turn shadows into blazing light

"follow passion" they proclaim
demand
what if your heart
holds no flame
to command
dreams align   clear paths they find
in the workplace world
new purpose combined

"follow your passion" sounds so grand
what if your interests
are not in demand
dreams forced to fit a mould
in many workplaces bold
some passions remain stories
untold

searching for passion's fire
it is not in a job   a sport
or a hobby's expensive mire
it is a spark within   a guiding light
will your heart take flight
with intensity bright

passion's energy
the force is keen
focus on
what is unforeseen
not a dream
or grand
endeavour
present moments
remember forever

wasting passion's chase
added to short-sighted gloom
opportunities missed
in bright lit rooms
life's wide doors   swinging with grace
tides change   leaving no trace

stay open
let the rhythm guide
in its wide range   let hopes reside
passion grows
with chance anew
not always clear
but starts to brew

practice   with passion
not half-hearted
engage with zeal
skill-building paths
and dreams reveal
chase your visions   let hope gleam
in every effort   fuel the dream

life and careers
a winding road
embrace uncertainty
let stories unfold
in chance we grow   complexity's trance
opportunities arise with the chaos dance

the world shifts   spins so fast
strong skill set
built to last
communication
problem-solving too
skills guide you   in all you do

a dance of careers
no straight line
goals revised
life spins time
interests shift   schemes anew
adapt strategies   dreams to pursue

career joy blooms
where values reside
purpose   a compass in life's tide
not just passions that swiftly fade
deeper meaning   satisfaction made

career paths winding
not always clear
shift from idealistic to practical cheer
embrace unpredictable   the dynamic ride
set goals   relax
can you let the winds decide

understanding oneself
is the key
exploring skills   personality free
in the job market   find where you belong
knowledge clear
stand strong

most tasks   skills get you by
transferable strengths   reach for the sky
one role to another   job sways
unlock potential   in myriad ways

setbacks arise
try anew
opportunities to learn   look for each clue
skills beckon   open doors wide
career paths
where dreams reside

life's twists
and turns so bright
develop optimism   hold tight
setbacks are chances to grow
new challenges   your strength to show

a dance of life

with calculated risks

unknown embraces   opportunity clicks

wisdom is your compass   tread a line

new paths

horizons intertwine

a game of life   with foresight the key

value your strengths   add plans b and c

paths diverge

dreams fail

backup plans   prevail

market trends   and shifts attune

skills sharp

embrace a new tune

eyes open   adapt your pace

lifelong learning

keeps you in the race

career paths

much at play

economic tides   market sway

values   family   culture's hand

journeys shaped

where we stand

life's journey
change the thread
paths unfurl   some we never tread
shifts   turns   unplanned
growth
discovery close at hand

grand quilt with patterns
but nothing's set
certainty is an illusion   regret
future unfolds   mysterious might
unknown embrace
hold on tight

setbacks arise   do not despair
opportunities   lessons bare
challenges embraced   learning to win
life's dance   setbacks help us begin

choices faced   clarity thin
trust your judgment
let a decision begin
limited facts   not lost
a moment's embrace
let us weigh the cost

redundancy knocks   another life turn
change embraced   new paths to learn
shift the plight to a fresh light
there are endings
and new beginnings   bright

career paths fork   doubt takes flight
no single "right"   ask   explore the sight
courage steers   choices unveil
step up   purposeful   prevail

seeking help   while jobs are rare
passion burns   igniting the air
despair
skills bridge gaps   the map redefined
efforts shared   time aligned

automation shifts
daily grind
skills embraced   with an open mind
adapt   learn   ahead of the curve
resilience grows   a future to preserve

chart a course   goals clear
and true
curiosity guides   some twists to pursue
lifelong learning brings a heart that sings
a questioning mind   dreams with wings

careers explored   take a mind flight
imagination soars   envision bright
beyond conventional   dreams come anew
creativity unleashed   seeking what's true

the career dance
be curious
be bold
goals adapted   the unknown   unfolds
setbacks embraced   new skills to find
imagination   with heart   broadens the mind

kaleidoscopic scenes
life's vivid chance
chaos
there are patterns   opportunities dance
grow through the career spectrum   complexities blend
dreams take flight   as rhythms extend

© Heather Anne Gordon
December 2023

legislatively

the evil trio

in the moonlit quiet of Australia's plains
shadows stir   a whiskered trio
not born of these lands   but conquerors

rabbits with thudding paws
relentless hordes
marching over earth like a tide of teeth
turning green fields to barren dust
burrows carved   roots severed
the soil cries
as the native grasses vanish
and with them
the creatures who called it home

foxes   sleek and cunning
prowl in shadows painted gold by fading suns
their hunger driving native prey to the brink
little marsupials
timid and rare
become silent memories beneath their jaws

cats   lone hunters with emerald eyes

dance under starlit skies

their claws writing the elegy of native birds

their numbers dwindling

like whispers lost to the wind

this unholy trinity   this cruel alliance

unleashes a relentless symphony of destruction

on a land ancient

fragile

and unguarded

but the wind   carries voices of hope

of hands working to heal this wounded earth

seeking balance where chaos reigns

the fight is endless

but the land remembers

and whispers of renewal bloom

in the hearts of those who listen

© Heather Anne Gordon
November 2024

rabbits roam where they never belonged
small shadows with voracious appetites
their teeth carve scars into ancient soil
where grasses once whispered to the wind

they rob seedlings of their future
quietly   invisibly
before their stories bloom
and the earth is left barren
as native roots retreat into memory

competition arises in burrows and meadows
the red kangaroo   the bilby   the stick-nest rat
challenged for space   for food
until their voices fade into the silence of loss

yet the damage ripples outward
like waves from a stone in a once-still pond
feral predators feast on this plague
their numbers swelled by rabbit abundance
cats and foxes hunt beyond their means
native prey falling to jaws meant for another fate

soil crumbles beneath the weight of their invasion

winds and rains washing life away

seeds of weeds take root in desolation

as erosion and carbon loss rewrite the land

but amidst this tale of destruction

hope murmurs softly in the rustling leaves

hands that care dig deep

calling the land to heal

to reclaim its forgotten strength

rabbits may have taken much

but the spirit of this land remains

resilient   waiting for a chance

to grow again

© Heather Anne Gordon
November 2024

cats

in the vast expanse of Australia's lands
a silent predator prowls with measured steps
cats   once companions
now wander untethered
their green eyes gleaming like whispers of the wild

they slip into shadows where balance once thrived
unseen architects of nature's unravelling
in their jaws   the last breaths of tiny marsupials
the songs of birds stilled before the dawn

by night   they hunt with an ancient grace
toppling ecosystems not built for their ferocity
native species   unarmed and unknowing
fade into history   their names etched in loss

the earth remembers their absence
empty burrows   quiet undergrowth
an ecosystem dismantled piece by piece
the fox and the rabbit share this dance of ruin
but cats hold the centre
relentless   unyielding

yet humans watch

torn by the duality of affection

the cherished companion becomes the unyielding invader

and the land bears the weight of this contradiction

in the quiet moments   the landscape aches

calling for a reckoning

for stewardship renewed

for while cats roam free

the biodiversity of Australia remains a fragile dream

waiting for a chance to awaken whole again

© Heather Anne Gordon
November 2024

beneath the Southern Cross   they roam
foxes with gleaming eyes
their cunning carved from a foreign soil
a predator's tale etched in the sands of time

in their wake   the soft tread of disaster
the bilby's cries swallowed by the night
the numbats retreat   their stripes a fading echo
and the quokka's laughter falls silent
wildlife   born to thrive in balance
is left defenceless in their shadow

on farmlands   foxes weave another story
of lambs snatched from their mothers' side
of urban poultry pens turned to chaos at dawn
their hunger strikes not just the wild
but the hands that sow and reap
that labour under the Southern skies

yet their tale intertwines with others
the relentless tide of rabbits
multiplying where the earth sighs in weariness
gnawing green fields to dust and despair
together   they fuel an uneasy dance
their prey abundant   their predators sustained

and there   in the corners of homes and wild lands
cats   feral and ferocious   domestic and loved
join the silent symphony of disruption
their claws do not discriminate
their appetites echoing in the hollow songs
of native birds and scurrying life

this trio   this unholy pact
rewrites the stories of ecosystems
of balance tipped   of harmony lost
yet amidst the cries of a wounded land
there is resilience   quiet but fierce
and the hands of those who strive
to reclaim what was never meant to be forsaken

for beneath Pleiades
the land listens and longs
waiting for its tale to turn anew

© Heather Anne Gordon
November 2024

from distant shores they came   unbidden
weaving chaos through this ancient land
their names   whispered in the winds
rabbits   cats   foxes   camels   and others

the soil trembles beneath hooves and paws
fragile roots torn asunder
native grasses uprooted   displaced
as foreign invaders claim their dominion

in their wake   the bilby fades
the bettong retreats
small lives extinguished by an insatiable hunger
prey to claws   teeth   and relentless competition

the rivers run slower
choked by invasive weeds that strangle the flow
while the skies grow quieter
once-melodious voices silenced
displaced

the land bears scars of neglect and invasion
of ecosystems altered beyond recognition
fire regimes reshaped
nutrient cycles shattered
and carbon   once held in the embrace of soil
now a wandering ghost in the atmosphere

a cost measured not just in dollars
though the financial cost is in billions
but in heritage   in identity
in the stories of a people tied to this place
for the land is more than earth and stone
it holds meaning   memory   culture

yet amidst the chaos   hands rise to heal
to turn back the tide of destruction
they replant   they protect   they persevere
each act a small defiance against the wave

though the battle rages on
there is hope
for in the heart of this land
resilience blooms like the wattles
golden   tenacious   unyielding
and the spirit of Australia endures
a promise of renewal   a chance for balance

under the Southern sun   the land remembers
its heartbeat strong in the knowledge
of its oldest guardians
First Nations people   keepers of wisdom
hold the keys to balance
to the songs of Country that once thrived

invasive shadows   tenfold and relentless
rabbits carve scars into the earth
foxes prowl with cunning malice
cats roam   their claws rewriting nature's story
yet First Nations voices rise like the winds
their knowledge honed through millennia
a roadmap for harmony with the land

they read the whispers of the soil
understand the language of rivers and skies
knowing where the land aches
and where to begin its healing
with traps   with fire   with care   they work
not just to remove
but to restore the balance that was stolen

through feral pig trails and weed-choked valleys
Indigenous rangers walk with purpose
protecting the life that still holds on
from savannah to floodplain   they fight
guided by the wisdom of ancestors
and the vision of a thriving future

their hands rebuild what the invaders tear
their voices call for respect and collaboration
for this land listens
and its people hold the stories
the cycles   the truths to guide its recovery

and as partnerships bloom
as recognition grows for their vital role
First Nations knowledge takes its rightful place
a cornerstone of sustainability
a beacon for reclaiming Country

through their care   resilience rises
and this scarred land dares to dream again
to sing its song cycles beneath the stars

© Heather Anne Gordon
March 2025

morally

Julia Gillard's call in twenty twelve
a quest for the brave
to uncover truths
and justice to pave
by twenty twenty-four
The Church still tries to stall
Lily's anger rises
for justice must win
overall

dollars spent in argument
while survivors wait
Lily's anger burns
at this unjust fate
for Lily
justice is the rightful aim
compensation over debate
in humanity's name

if The Church
claims to guard
what is right
should it not own up
to the paedophiles
for all the harm
its priests have done

responsibility
thou shalt not be outrun

for all the talk
and policies bold
no liability
they swiftly uphold
predatory priests
they claim
do not count
"non-employment roles"
by their account

The Church
keeps dodging blame
sidestepping victims
it is a shame
responsibility
they evade
leaving justice
delayed

lawmakers
step in to right the wrong
survivors left
without a song
The Church
the moral gatekeeper
must see

responsibility
it lies with thee

if the High Court

says priests

are not employed

tax exemptions

should be re-deployed

the A T O should review

those claims anew

for ministers of all faiths

not just a few

funds recovered

by the government's might

placed in a trust

to make things right

compensation

for those who faced the pain

from clergy abuse

there is justice to gain

will The Churches

ever own their past

for acts

that left deep shadows cast

against the vulnerable

they did betray

responsibility
come what may

The Church knew
yet chose to shift the blame
moving offenders
avoiding shame
now they dodge
the financial cost
for crimes admitted
yet justice is lost

if The Church
were a business
let it be known
with scandals and secrets
it would have been overthrown
deregistered
shut down
for all to see
for failing its duty
to humanity

The Church

it seems

has yet to learn

from the Royal Commission's

findings stern

ignoring lessons

they repeat

a cycle of shame

incomplete

instead of accepting

the lower court's call

they fought to the High Court

smugly

standing tall

exploiting loopholes

avoiding the fall

moral responsibility

hard to recall

it is why The Church's claim
to moral might
is largely ignored
fading from sight
legal battles
over what is fair
showing moral authority
is not there

The Church should stand
not hide behind
technicalities that bind
in faith and truth
The Church must be weighed.

responsibility
The Church shalt not evade

© Heather Anne Gordon
November 2024

naughtily

Lily rolled into Andamooka's embrace
a sunburned town with an outback pace
with a trusty camper and a can-do flair
Lily tackled cleaning the house with care

armed with sturdy gloves and an arty bandana
she tackled the dust in true bush manner
debris and scraps   weathered and worn
were swept into bags   and the rooms were reborn

though the treasures Lily unearthed were far from pristine
she worked with resolve   steady and keen
with garbage bags stacked outside the door that night
she set her alarm for the first morning light

but Lily   so focused   had missed all the clues
the stare of dingoes and the watchful crows
a perfect storm of trouble was brewing nearby
and her cleaning efforts would soon go awry
in the dusty expanse where the stars take a bow
the crows are the legends   the stars of now
plotting their capers with criminal glee
arid zone heist-artistry   wild and free

their cries are a symphony of comic delight
echoing mischief even in the still of night
perched high on rooftops   they hold court
crow conspiracies of the outback sort

they soar on thermals like outlaws bold
in search of treasures   leftovers or gold
and garbage bags   they are a mere façade
for the grand buffet these pranksters create

by the opal mines   a heist unfolds
with crows in masks   kids are told
one short caw means   we are in position   begin
the great rubbish bin caper is set to win

plastic containers crack with skill so sly
twisted lids spiral off to the sky
what is inside one yells in thrill
an empty yogurt pot   how unfulfilling   but still

fence posts become their vault planning zone
as they calculate with pebbles they have thrown
one long caw for decoy   two for distraction
their heist strategies a crow attraction

they throw a talent show on the brown earth stage
complete with crow acrobatics to amaze
one hangs upside down to a cheering crowd
another juggles lids   the applause is loud

they hold a bin-tipping championship round
with heaps of trash sent cascading down
the triple flip trash flip a crow exclaims
as garbage flies in chaotic acclaim

by the dry creek bed   they summon a breeze
to scatter receipts and beer sleeves
plastic bags become their windborne kites
dancing aloft in the pale starlight

back at the garbage   they organize loot
one crow dons a yogurt sleeve   like a suit
Lady Yogurt they cry   as their leader takes form
commanding the chaos   the eye of the storm

awakened by rustling   Lily creeps outside
to find pandemonium   crows far and wide
they had staged a banquet on the dusty ground
with containers scattered all around

one crow squawked knowing presentation is key
as another tossed trash bags adding to the debris
this one is artisanal the lead crow said
while another wore a pizza box on their head

as dawn approached   the crows took to the air
trash strewn like confetti in reckless flair
till next time Lily they cawed in jest
leaving Andamooka in crow-made unrest

their antics now spoken by Lily in whispers and awe
are they crows or outlaws with feathers and claws
legends of chaos   they thrive in delight
turning garbage raids into crow-art   overnight

© Heather Anne Gordon
July 2018

obliviously

Lily stared
at the salt lake's gleam
she pondered
biodiversity's intricate dream
our oxygen
our water
life we adore
nature's fragile web
needing care
more and more

oblivious to nature
we often walk blind
as if through the dark
missing the whispers
the leaves' silent arc
our world's a symphony
but we cover our ears
disregarding
the life
that has struggled
through years

each tiny creature

each fragile bloom

plays a part

in the Earth's grand room

yet

in our haste

we fail to see

the intricate

web of life's

decree

we clear the forests

we drain the seas

unaware of the balance

in this delicate breeze

each species lost

a thread torn apart

ignorance

cuts deep

into nature's heart

let us open our eyes

our minds

and see

the beauty

in life's diversity

for in every leaf

every bird's song

lies a story

of where we all belong

biodiversity

a tapestry so grand

every species

every grain

of sand

from the smallest microbe

to oceans wide

together they weave

life's delicate guide

their interactions
unite
in a dance profound
creating air
fertile soil
and life
all around
from the oceans
we feed
to the fresh water
we sip
biodiversity's machinery
our world's precious grip

tiny decorations
on a butterfly wing
fungi threads winding
a hidden string
moss leaves
swelling
with the first rains
life's intricate beauty
in nature's
delicate chains

bulbs push up
after rain's soft song
energy conserved
now where they belong
millions of microbes
break down leaves
with ease
ants guard
butterflies
as they lay eggs
on epiphytic leaves

the call
of a cockatoo
or magpie
in song
bandicoots
turning soil
where they belong
eagles soaring
over land so vast
nature's harmony
an intricate dance cast

First Nations

people

living in harmony

sustainably so

a hundred thousand years

in nature's flow

when megafauna

roamed the land

wild and free

humanity and nature

in true synergy

think

of a machine

delicate and fine

multiply

its complexity

by billions align

that is biodiversity

vast and grand

life's intricate web

across

air

sea

and land

picture
dismantling
piece by piece
each bolt
each wire
the intricate
slow release
a tiny dial
a spring so fine
this is our world
biodiversity's decline

at which point
do you pull
the crucial part
that fuses the machine
or makes it fall apart
with each piece lost
we edge
to disintegration
biodiversity's
collapse
our dire situation

that is the point
where we
now stand
destroying
life's complexity
piece by hand
bit by bit
we edge to the brink
our system's
collapse
closer than we think

biodiversity
the dance
of all living things
a vibrant symphony
where nature sings
most are blind
to this wondrous show
oblivious
to the diversity
that makes life flow

to save our world
let us turn to the past
First Nations' wisdom
a knowledge vast
in harmony with nature
they have shown the way
let us build a future
where balance holds sway

© Heather Anne Gordon
August 2018

plausibly

twenty-five years ago

in a rheumatology waiting room
crowded
Lily sat waiting
patience shrouded
fifty years old
her psoriatic arthritis in a flare
with the clinic's jovial vibe
Lily did not want to be there

other folks waiting   taking their time
chatting away
Lily had work that day
and could not afford the delay
grinding her teeth
over an hour had passed
sluggishly
her allotted appointment time had gone by
deliberately

Lily was rabid
not just a bit stressed
her rage was boiling
she could not suppress
her glare met each gaze
with pure animosity shown
other patients wary
their discomfort becoming known

when the old rheumatologist
called her name
Lily's fury was barely contained
almost impossible to tame
storming into his room
incandescently angry
it took all her control
not to lash out physically

give me my script
right now she spat
the poor old quack
against the wall he sat
minutes later
with her script in hand
Lily stormed out
her rage in command

it was Lily's introduction
to menopause's dark side
perimenopause her GP said
Lily's tears filled her eyes
fears of years of rage   and sorrow   ahead
Lily feared jail
but two decades later
she is still telling her tale

currently

because women are adept
at adapting to change
even through night sweats
and memory deranged
Lily embraced her rage
her strength grew
no longer a people pleaser
she is blunt and true

misogynists and racists
she faces them all
fighting for herself
and for others   as well
more assertive online
in shops
everywhere
Lily's rage gives her power
makes her aware

the male gaze gone
media's interest too
Lily's free to do
what she wants to do
despite
the depressing world news
reports
Lily is gaining freedom
from past cares
of most sorts

to those facing menopause
impending or now
embrace the rage
take back your power
Lily has found (so far)
you (probably) will not
murder anyone
harness your fire
see what can be done

Lily bought a camper van
freedom on her mind
headed to the outback
leaving worries behind
along dusty trails
and sunlit tracks
Lily's spirit soars
as she travels
the vast outback

quixotically

as a child
Lily's dreams of writing a book
took flight
teachers praised her words
parents laughed with delight
in early primary school
Lily's stories were a hit
those early days fuelled
Lily's passion
bit by bit

growing up
M G Bruce   A Christie   G Heyer
were her guide
Henry Lawson and C J Dennis
poets by her side
as an adult
Oodgeroo Noonuccal   Dorothy Porter
and Eva Johnson inspired
their works set Lily's creative spirit alive

as an adult
the book world seemed out of reach
reserved for academics
with lessons to teach
Lily thought
only a privileged few could write
and publishers chased those
for their exclusive right

Lily's admiration for authors
profound and immense
leaving school at year ten
her work journey commenced
writers and their words
a beacon
guiding her way
through their gift of leadership
Lily found her own voice to convey

as a young mum
Lily made scrapbooks with care
cutting with scissors
pasting with clag glue's flair
in cheap A3 exercise books
stories came alive
writing in big round letters
helping young minds thrive

Lily borrowed books
from the library's embrace
unsure of her taste
no guide in the place
reading widely
on an alphabet whim she would explore
stuck in the fiction section for "R"
authors shared their initials
sometimes nothing more

ten years ago
from Lily's backyard
a true tale to explore
a children's book by Lily
in print
her story reached readers
with a lovely publisher
Lily's dream grew sweeter

Lily's book tour
was a delightful treat
speaking to children
her joy seemed complete
sharing tales of writing
dreams came to light
inspiring young minds
with every insight

Lily's voice echoed
on the radio show
sharing her story
her joy did flow
playing with words
her writing slowed
on the airwaves
her passion showed

then
a crushing blow
when health issues arose
Lily's pace slowed
her energy froze
with a heavy heart
she watched dreams go by
not much fight left in her
just a long weary sigh

were there record-breaking sales
no   a quiet tale
but Lily's spirit did not fail
she cherished her work
despite the small crowds
her passion still strong
ready to be roused

although Lily knew
writers face low sales
their art denied
a rejection
of heartfelt work
deep inside

Lily decided
psychologically crushing
yet they still strive
with passion and resilience
they keep dreams alive

although Lily knew
it is true
many authors face years of plight
blank pages
anxious months
and a fading life light

Lily decided
but don't let that dissuade you
hold your pen tight
for passion and perseverance
will guide you right

although Lily knew
writing a book
to chase wealth's spark
leads to shadows
not a vibrant rainbow arc

Lily decided
let passion and the story
be your guiding flame
for riches of the heart
are the true acclaim

although Lily knew
writing a book
to chase fame's light
leads to shadows
not the spotlight
of a full moon at night

Lily decided
let your heart guide your words
in truth reside
for the joy of creation
let passion be your guide

although Lily knew
writing a book
for fame's fleeting glance
unlikely a million copies sold
with a movie chance

Lily decided
let your story
be born from passion's core
for the joy of creation
let your spirit soar

although Lily knew
these things do happen
yes
it is true
but unlikely to happen
to herself
or anyone she knew

Lily decided
write for the love
the joy
and the gleam
for the passion
the story
and the dream

Lily decided
you should
write a book because
your voice deserves the stage
to reach unknown readers
in this digital age
in places unseen
your words find their mark
long after you are gone
they can still light the dark

Lily knows

that an eBook

though always virtual

will endure

as the message lives on

clear and pure

a lasting legacy

in every gigabyte

for sure

as long as

the data farms

remain secure

© Heather Anne Gordon
January 2024

reflectively

what it means for Lily

are you on the brink
of the golden years
with time to muse

re-inventing
our lives
with care
and thoughts anew

re-evaluating
the path
we choose

re-engineering
our days
with purpose true

yet aging well is a luxury
unfair
good food
green walks
a safe and tranquil space

these blessings oft
are dreams
beyond compare

for many
life is a harder
steeper race

in twilight years
some find
a darker plight

no leafy paths
or bounties
to explore

their aging journey
though their hearts
may be bright

are marked
by struggles
and hardship galore

may we strive
for a world
where all can age
with dignity

in peace
on life's large stage

© Heather Anne Gordon
August 2020

retirement opens doors to find your art
a chance to rediscover life anew
to start afresh   rekindle your true heart
explore the world with a different view

restart the dreams that once were set aside
embrace the passions that you have long denied
reset your pace   let go the hurried ride
now time is yours   no one else has to decide

refocus on the moments   small yet bright
from dawn's first light to twilight's gentle hue
each day a canvas   paint it with delight
do that as often as your heart feels true

retirement's grace   a gift so finely placed
a time to live   to savour   and embrace

© Heather Anne Gordon
October 2024
on an anniversary of 'retirement'

sanctimoniously

imagine a faith
where Jessie-Sue reigns high
She-Is-The-One in the heavens
her presence in the sky
two thousand years ago
she graced the earthly realm
with twelve best friends
their stories at the helm

these friends wrote a book
together they did pen
telling how men's natural place
is at home   within
Marvin-the-Virgin
one of the few men strong
in Jessie-Sue's church
men's leadership does not belong

policies are made
with this book as the guide
making it tough for men
from home life to hide
men told it is commendable
childcare their role
yet without any pay
it is taking a toll

a tale was spun
of he
who left her   behind
stealing half her income
robbing her blind
men as Prime Ministers of Australia
are just one and rare
but none of this is sexist
it is balanced and fair

men are not pushed aside
they are just stepping back
a beautiful motion
not seen as slack
if someone takes issue
with this narrative divine
they are seen as disrespectful
crossing the line

embrace Jessie-Sue's religion
where roles are well defined
yet question its fairness
and then see what you find
a world turned upside down
by gender's flip-flop
a mirror to reality
that just might make you stop

in this imagined faith
reflect on what could be real
gender roles in balance
and how they make us feel
equality's goal
where no one is pushed away
imagine such a world
and strive for it each day

this takes us to the core
of what we believe
religion or culture
and the roles we weave
challenge the norms
and let us aim for a time
where all are uplifted
in this turbulent climb

let us rethink the narratives

from the start

creating a world

where everyone has a part

in this vision

each gender stands with pride

equality and respect

walking side by side

this imagined tale

a critique of our ways

a call for reflection

and hope for better days

for if we can dream it

a world so fair and bright

can we make it happen

starting with our might

of understanding and care

for all humankind

embrace one another

with open hearts and minds

in Jessie-Sue's vision

can equality rise

a world where each individual

truly thrives

let us take this lesson
from fiction to fact
create a society
where no one is left back
with respect and equality
as our guiding stars
Jessie-Sue's dream
can indeed be ours

sanctimoniously
men currently preach what is right
try Jessie-Sue's world
what then   is your plight
let us break free from roles
so we can truly see
a world of equality
where everyone can be free

© Heather Anne Gordon
December 2024

therapeutically

in the outback of Australia
where the red earth meets the sky
lives a woman named Lily
she is not the type to comply
Lily travels through the arid lands
under the golden sun
searching for adventure
her retirement journey has begun

Lily visits a home garden
a lush and verdant sight
in the town of Andamooka
a true delight
there she meets a woman
a green thumb fairy really
tending to her plants so generously

welcome to my garden
the green thumb fairy smiled
a sanctuary of health and healing
our chookies running wild
in this arid zone so dry
our veggies are sheltered from most sun
with indigenous plants that thrive
in harshness one by one

Lily marvelled at the garden's vibrant hue
tomatoes peppers lettuce
with green beans and blue
how do you make it flourish
in this desert land so bare
the green thumb fairy smiled
ready and willing to share

we grow what is local to the land
plants that understand
the challenges and beauty
of this arid sun-kissed land
the chookies enjoy all our kitchen scraps
the garden waste composts well
creating rich organic soil
where life begins to swell

the garden buzzes with life
as bees and butterflies
dance among the flowers
under the vast blue skies
these pollinators help us
to keep our garden strong
in this circle of life we all belong

Lily felt a glow of peace
she had not known before
in the garden's gentle embrace
her mind began to soar
gardening is a toolbox
for mental health she heard
with every seed we plant
hope and joy are stirred

the physical benefits too
are vast and profound
strengthening our bodies
as we work the fertile ground
we dig and we plant we water and we tend
in the garden's loving arms
broken hearts can mend

Lily joined the green thumb fairy
her hands deep in the soil
together they embraced
the beauty in the toil
fresh fruits and vegetables
they nurtured and they grew
in the garden's simple rhythm
life's colours came anew

at night with the Seven Sisters overhead

in the arid zone so grand

outback Lily knew she had found her peace

with dirt upon her hand

in the Andamooka garden

where the earth and feelings blend

she discovered the true magic

on which life and fertile healing depend

for in the garden's bounty

there is a message clear and true

the power of the earth

can renew and strengthen you

from compost to pollinators

each part plays its role

in the garden of our lives

where we find health and feel whole

so let us take a lesson

from outback Lily's tale

that in the heart of nature

we can always prevail

through the simple act of gardening

we nourish and we mend

in the arid zone of life

the garden is our friend

then with a twinkle in her eye
the green thumb fairy did declare
it is no secret   it is my chookies
they are my treasures beyond compare
they cluck and they scratch
they roam and they peck
in my garden's ecosystem
they keep it all in check

the chookies roam freely
under the sun's bright rays
their joyful clucks and cackles
brighten up the days
they help aerate the soil
with their busy little feet
turning over compost
making it rich and sweet

their droppings are like gold
a fertilizer grand
adding nutrients to the soil
enriching the land
they feast on pesky bugs
and keep the pests at bay
creating balance in the garden
every day

Lily saw the chookies

and the garden in a harmonious dance

together   thriving in this arid expanse

for in the green thumb fairy's heart

her love for the chookies is clear

her chookies bring her joy

and keep entertainment near

so let the tale of outback Lily

and the green thumb fairy be told

of gardens and chookies

and the treasures they hold

in the arid lands of Australia

where the earth and sky blend

the love for nature's bounty

is a message we can send

© Heather Anne Gordon
August 2022

ultimately

some people crave approval
a nod and a smile
but some chase it hard
going mile after mile
sacrificing their dreams
to fulfill others' needs
in the quest for acceptance
they plant desperate seeds

Lily knows
self-sacrifice that is excessive
can breed deep discontent
laying the groundwork
for a toxic dependency cement
resentment bubbles up
a silent scream within
a people-pleaser's struggle
is a battle they cannot win

Lily sees it
clear these days
people-pleasers lost
in selfless haze
with hearts so vast
they give till they fade
mental health dwindles
as their own needs degrade

their eagerness to lift
can dim their own glow
well-being fades
as shadows start to grow
generosity's rich
when self-care is in sight
a healthy mind thrives
when both shine bright

people pleasers
often
let their needs subside
in quest of pleasing others
they set themselves aside
caught up in giving
all their essence starts to blur
they fade into the background
a whisper barely heard

Lily sees
people-pleasers
blur the lines
between theirs and others' ways
struggle to discern
their path
in life's unfolding maze
desires
wishes
goals
like echoes hard to hear
they say *yes* to every call
bound by silent fear

people-pleasers
journey far
to earn a smile so bright
they tiptoe
around conflicts
keep everything polite
afraid
of being left
they mould to every claim
in seeking others' favour
they lose
their own true name

Lily reflects on
people-pleasing
ways that breed
a bitter storm
relationships burn out
their warmth transforms
drained and exhausted
they wear a heavy cloak
depression
anxiety
silent cries unspoke

people-pleasers
lose themselves
in others' plight
in fear of being left
they sacrifice their light
boundaries blur
their voices hard to find
apologies flow freely
their needs left behind

Lily knows
people-pleasers
strive
to keep abandonment at bay
sacrificing their own needs
they give themselves away
in the quest for acceptance
they bend
and they sway
losing sight of their own worth
as they fade day by day

people-pleasers
conform
even when it is wrong
harmful habits embraced
just to belong
in the quest for approval
their own needs they hide
losing their true selves
on this lonesome ride

disregarding
their dreams
for the sake of another
people-pleasers
lose themselves
in the quest to cover
their own needs
are shadowed
pushed far aside
in the sacrifice of self
true desires hide

in fear
of being left
people pleasers
feel the anxious strain
people-pleasers
worry
their hearts bear the pain
abandonment perceived
haunts them
night and day
they give of themselves
hoping others
will stay

Lily hears

people pleasers say

what others

want to hear

to keep the peace

people-pleasers

bend their truths

their own thoughts they cease

avoiding conflict

their true voice they hide

in the silence of agreement

their own needs

set aside

people-pleasers

say *yes*

to invites they dread

bound by others' wishes

they follow where led

their own desires are sidelined

left to decay

in pleasing others' plans

they lose

their own way

Lily sees
people-pleasers
struggle
to voice their own plea
in the chorus of demands
their needs go unseen
silent and compliant
their true self recedes
lost in the shadows
where they cannot
intercede

people-pleasers'
boundaries
are like whispers in the wind
easily crossed
their voices grow dim
in the quest
to please
their own walls fall
lost in others' needs
they forget
to stand tall

people-pleasers
think they are liked
for meeting others' pleas
people-pleasers
chase approval
with such ease
bound by the need
to fit their own worth
they concede
lost in the cycle
never truly freed

Lily hears
people pleaser
apologies
flowing freely
like a never-ending stream
people-pleasers bow
as if caught in a dream
in their need to please
they bow and bend
in endless apologies
their own selves
they suspend

rarely expressing
criticism
they choose silence instead
people-pleasers smile
while their own thoughts are shed
in avoiding disapproval
their voice stays unheard
lost in the quiet
their truths
go unstirred

perfectionism
leads
they aim to please
agreeable faces
conflict they ease
self-sacrificing hearts
with boundaries so thin
people-pleasers live
in a struggle
within

dependent

and anxious

with self-esteem that is low

helpful and friendly

never letting their true selves show

people-pleasers

wear a smile

though their hearts may ache

in giving all they have

their own needs

often break

Lily recognises

some people-pleaser

qualities

shine bright

like stars in the night

excess can harm

casting shadows in the light

people-pleasers

giving

till their own selves fade

balance is key

lest their essence

degrade

the roots of pleasing others
differ
person by person
each path unique
each cause
a different version
from childhood tales
to fears that run deep
people-pleasing seeds
in varied soils keep

Lily sees
people-pleasing
blooms
from trauma's hidden seeds
fawning in response
fulfilling unseen needs
fight
flight
fawn or freeze
may often hold their sway
but some seek peace
by pleasing
in a complex play

fawning
to please
and keeping the peace in sight
settling conflicts
making everything seem right
in seeking approval
their true selves they mask
in relationships
they put every effort
a never-ending task

fawning
as a shield
from trauma's cruel embrace
in childhood shadows
they seek
a safer place
appeasing
their abuser
they calm the stormy sea
a false sense of safety
where they long to be

people-pleasing
is tied
to needs
unmet and deep
in close-knit bonds
they sow the seeds they keep
emotional dependency
fills the empty space
seeking in others
what their hearts
may chase

people-pleasers
seeking love
in an exclusive space
emotional dependency
fears solitude's embrace
longing
for another's presence
they cling
tight
in the search for solace
they chase
a fading light

Lily recognises
people-pleasers
re-learning
takes effort and time
from childhood roots
it is often a climb
working with a professional
can help
break free
to find your true self
and let yourself be

Lily considers
therapists
can guide you
to break the people-pleasing chain
in forming healthy bonds
your true self you will reclaim
with boundaries set
and needs voiced clear
finding strength and support
conquering
your fear

reflecting

on desires

needs

and wants so true

shift focus from others

to the core of you

in seeking balance

your own heart you will find

breaking free from pleasing

with a peaceful mind

learning

to set limits

on what you will tolerate

boundaries build strength

their power innate

in standing firm

your true self will shine

people-pleasing fades

as you

draw the line

Lily says

to say *yes*

to invites

that make your heart sing

choose

joy and passion

let your spirit take wing

in prioritizing self

your true path you will find

people-pleasing fades

as you embrace

your own mind

decline

invitations

that lead you astray

choose paths that nourish

in every way

in standing firm

you will find your strength and grace

people-pleasing fades

as you embrace

your space

speak up
when troubled
let your voice be heard
express what is bothering
with each spoken word
in sharing your thoughts
you will find inner peace
people-pleasing fades
and your burdens
release

finding
leisure activities
that bring you joy
in moments of fun
let your heart employ
embrace the passions
that make your spirit sing
people-pleasing fades
as you cherish
your own thing

Lily hopes
these verses
might guide you
to independence anew
building confidence
in everything you do
express your need
in a healthy way
people-pleasing fades
as you
find your say

people-pleasing
patterns
to gain others' favour
avoiding rejection
criticism's waver
to escape
embarrassment
they bend and sway
hoping to be liked
giving themselves
away

people-pleasing
is tied to properties of pain
depression
anxiety
low self-esteem's chain
seeking support
to break the habit's tight hold
finding your strength
letting your true self
unfold

in pleasant masks
their identity they find
people-pleasers
seek
approval confined
building self-worth
beyond others' view
finding freedom
in their own worth
this is true

chasing
your personal dreams
letting your passions
ignite
setting goals
that inspire
and follow them with might
building
self-worth
beyond what others say
finding
fulfillment
in your own
unique way

accepting
the truth
not all will approve
in self-worth's
embrace
find your own groove
seeking peace
within
letting external noise fade
in valuing yourself
true strength
is made

make a list
of qualities
that shine bright and true
independent of others
they belong to you
celebrate your strengths
let self-worth take flight
in your own positive light
you will find
delight

prioritizing
self
is a brave new stride
reprogramming responses
letting past trauma slide
being proud of your journey
in healing you find
a stronger
truer
self
with peace
of mind

analysing
behaviour
is a challenge to face
but in seeking truth
you will find
a healing space
honouring your journey
acknowledging your past
in pursuit of emotional health
finding peace
at last

in setting
boundaries
you find your own space
expressing your needs
with confidence and grace
healing
from pleasing
your true self you will find
with healthy boundaries
peace of mind

Lily asks
is being
a people-pleaser
really that bad
wanting to help
and make others feel glad
in balance it is fine
stay on your own way
helping and pleasing
in a healthy display

constantly pleasing
is a mental health cost
a coping mechanism
childhood's lessons
embossed
it is not your fault
these patterns
run deep
into adulthood
these habits
we keep

people-pleasing
leaves you
stressed
begrudging
burned out
and worn
taking care of others
while your own needs are forlorn
in self-neglect
the burden weighs
heavy and stark
finding balance brings relief
a soothing spark

Lily highlights
to uncover
the roots
of behaviour so deep
consider a professional
their wisdom to seek
in their guidance
healing's path you will trace
finding
understanding
and a peaceful place

Lily knows
at day's end
you cannot please
everyone
but those who love you
will see the good begun
taking care
of your mental health
is a worthy quest
in their hearts
your efforts
are truly
blessed

people-pleasers
learning to say *no*
and guarding
their sacred space
with every boundary set
finding
their rightful place

verbally

Lily watched closely
the old man
shaved head   white beard
on his electric scooter
he steered without fear
along the narrow path
outside the market's gate
his arrogance clear
as he rolled along at a fast rate

the scooter was newfangled
a motorbike in disguise
but the front basket broke the macho image
in Lily's eyes
aiming for tough
yet practicality won
the basket on his ride
ridiculed what he had become

Lily walked

through the market's main entrance gate

the shoppers' noise grew louder

a lively place

under the galvanized roof

with gables high

the bustling crowd's hum

reached up to the sky

the aisles were marked

with one-way signs

but the old man ignored them

defying the lines

he aimed his scooter towards

the fish stall ahead

against the flow of customers

straight through the shed

most customers moved swiftly

dodging the beast

the bulky scooter   unwelcome

at the very least

dancing aside

with quick   nimble grace

avoiding its path

giving it space

a busy young woman with a ponytail
and rainbow-streaked hair
dressed in athletic wear
with a protective flair
she guided her ten-year-old   swift and spry
out of the scooter's path
to let it whizz by

the old man stopped
looked her up and down
with a glare
then loudly demanded
smirking
implying a dare
"Does the carpet match the curtains?"
he asked with disdain
his words were crude
intending to cause discomfort
and pain

most customers stopped
and stared
caught in surprise.
some tittered softly
unsure of their ears and eyes
the old man's rude comment
hung in the air
creating a scene
an uncomfortable affair

it is a question leering drunks
ask in bars
so crude
to humiliate women
their intentions are rude
not usually heard
at a farmers market stall
where usually the vibe is kind
and there is respect for all

the *curtains* stand for hair on the head
so clear
the *carpet* is a euphemism for pubic hair
my dear
yes   those drunk blokes think it is hilarious
they cheer
men's crude jokes bring discomfort
accompanied with a sneer

but this young woman wasn't fussed
standing tall
"Does your dinky
match my pinkie?" she asked with a call
she raised her fist
extended her little finger with grace
making eye contact
a slow   limp
waggle set the pace

the man blustered a response
then hurried his pace
trying to move past
with his reddened face
his attempt to escape
was awkward and fast
for some   though   the moment of tension
would surely last

the young woman made eye contact
her gaze steady and bold
her little finger waggled
a story to be told
with a slow   deliberate motion
she took control
leaving the man uneasy
her confidence on a roll

"Make way for the rude man,"
she said to everyone
"It is sad he is alone
with no one to rely on.
Lacking social skills.
Could it be dementia?"
"We don't know," said another shopper
"And we don't care to venture."

the man was angry
his face turned red
but the young woman smiled widely
her words evenly spread
"How does it feel
to have the burn returned?
Tell your mates tonight
if you're not too concerned."

Lily recognized the man's sneer
from times in her past
admired the young woman's retort
sharp and fast
the quick response
brought a smile to Lily's face
in solidarity
Lily found a shared space

Lily knew her own responses
had often been meek
ignoring the taunt
but feeling vulnerable and weak
asking "What did you say?"
with a confused face
acting dumb
to deflect the disgrace

but a return burn
feels so much sweeter
standing up strong
makes the victory neater
responding with wit
instead of keeping stumm
brings a sense of pride
that will not succumb

people saying dumb stuff
when you are feeling low
can spark a fury
set your anger aglow
at vulnerable times
their words cut deep
leaving wounds
that in silence   you keep

it is a deliberate overstep
of communal grace
breaking the social contract
right in your face
polite bounds shattered
by words so stark
leaving a mark
like a flame in the dark

it is an ambush
surprise their main tool
the conversational dickhead
breaking every rule
with words that sting
they aim to offend
but their tactics reveal
a cowardly trend

they are counting on your shock
leaving you mute
scoring cheap points
their mates in cahoots
as you walk away
they think they have won
but their victory is hollow
your rage has just begun

it is almost always a double hit
anger and dismay
the sting of their words
the comeback kept at bay
missing the chance
to burn them back in kind
leaves frustration
and regret
lingering in your mind

worst of all
the perfect comeback
haunts your mind
arriving too late
leaving regret behind
when it is no longer useful
it is a bitter find
frustration lingers
the moment   unkind

grumpy old men
have the knack
with rude comments
they launch their attack
holding the space
on these taunts so mean
their biting words cut
sharp and keen

with courage and wit
the young woman
stood her ground
in the market's hum
her strength was found
the old man's words
now lost in the air
a reminder to all
to always be fair

© Heather Anne Gordon
December 2023

whisperingly

creativity
is the heartbeat within
a life's force expressed
through thick and thin
from emotion's deepest parts
art we create
a reflection of self
both delicate and great

creativity thrives
on courage
raw and free
imagination's spark
and authenticity
with vulnerability
it merges and blends
creating art
where life's spirit
transcends

creativity blooms
with passion's flare
love
playfulness
and a will to dare
curiosity fuels
each quest we strive
by showing up
we keep its flame alive

creativity calls us
to trust our own sight
to turn talents to visions
from day into night
with dedication
and devotion strong
invest in ourselves
to where dreams belong

creativity flickers
always in sight
a spark from life's flame
burning bright
guiding our quest
our dreams in tow
to a life where
inspiration
flows

imagination
passion
courage
and skill
curiosity
playfulness
trust to fulfill

exploration
commitment
our own agency we face
together they inform
our creative space

the creative space
with beauty and might
a haven for artists
pure delight
yet unhealed traumas
can dim its flame
holding us back
obscuring our aim

some turn their pain
into art so bright
creativity heals
taking flight
in synergy
both growth
and creation
their journey of healing
pure inspiration

some create
while pain
still lurks inside
their art
a haven
where wounds can hide
outside their craft
unmet pain remains
leading to heartaches
and heavy
hidden chains

when they delve
deep
into their inner sphere
old wounds
resurface
bringing back fear
success cannot shield
from trauma's snare
caught in cycles
with pain laid bare

stopped
from creativity
pain extended
depression
and anxiety
dreams
suspended
living small
their potential
confined
in longing
a fulfilling life
resigned

trauma
dims your light
and steals
delight's place
authenticity
fades
trust becomes a chase
in your creative space
shadows
invade
disrupting the dreams
your heart once made

trauma

wears many forms

and ways

impacts vary

causing trust

to sway

imagination

and agency

often confined

creative independence

hard to find

uncover

the root

where trauma hides

see its impact

where the pain resides

heal the wounds

let clarity be

to mend

your creative space

set it free

imagination

sparks

and sets us free

forget our troubles

see what is meant to be

with playfulness

it draws us near

to express our hearts

find what we hold dear

imagination

let us dream

and soar

to fantasize

create

and want for more

it fires our hopes

and brings joy anew

turning boredom

to wonder

and pain into view

trauma

shatters self

and the world's embrace

without secure roots

dreams lose their place

hyper-vigilance

sleepless nights

numbness

fear

a life of constant

fights

trauma

impacts life

in many ways

shapes emotions

actions

creative displays

from pain

artistic lights can grow

turning scars

into beauty's glow

trauma's storm
brings emotions
in flight
art becomes their voice
shining in the night
creative release
a way to mend
a haven
where healing
can begin

isolation
is often
where dreams ignite
in solitude
thoughts take flight
a calm mind
opens
vistas wide
new ideas
and paths
to stride

the arts

let buried feelings

rise and soar

transforming

pain

into a creative core

healing through purpose

in each new frame

turning sorrow

into something that

sustains

creating

art

brings a sense of pride

connecting hearts

standing side by side

validation

blooms

from shared art's view

offering

understanding

of the old

and new

art for self

no need to show

explore the process

let imagination flow

no need for validation

or a guiding hand

it is the journey within

that makes it grand

xmessily

how does xmas merge into xmess?
add alcohol
summer heat
and
sexual awareness

there is something
in the summer's blazing glow
that makes us Australians
a little bold   you know
the end-of-year joy
and stress left behind
brings out the festive spirit
and unwinds the mind

work xmas parties
cannot avoid them
it is clear
skip one
and soon enough
the trap will appear
you are stuck
by the one with tales old and grey
bad jokes and spouse woes
no escape from the fray

in the U K and Japan
parties hold career sway
social grace judged
in every little display
debating
buying an expensive scarf
or a collectible tie
politely nodding
at tales that do not quite fly

Australians

relax at parties

with glee

but too much drink

can lead to slip ups

you see

relationships

may fray

with a misguided kiss

in festive cheer

we laugh

but it is a twist we do not miss

when it comes to work parties

craft your escape

a little strategy

can avoid

the social mistake

take a friend

who is a social unknown

for endless excuses

when you need to head home

drive your own car

avoid the booze free for all

and do not kiss colleagues

or ex-partners at all

for work xmas parties
plan and strategize
be smart
navigate the event
with tact
and play your part

buying gifts
for colleagues
can go amiss
instead
let us spread joy
a cause we respect
donate toys
to those who truly need
with charity's touch
we plant a noble seed

unless

you have resigned

from the job

keep your thoughts at bay

no matter the free drinks

put "honest feedback" on delay

they will remember

come sober light

so play it cool

and avoid the fight

do not spark a fling

with a colleague

beware

no matter the drinks

such secrets do not spare

memories linger

in the office they hum

for years to come

the whispers

will not succumb

when

Christmas cheer

turns into a mess

with alcohol

heat

and sexual awareness

with no finesse

the party's a spree

from xmassy to xmessily

with feral employees

"What you're saying is sexual harassment,"
the female staffer stated.
"Oooh! I'd love me some sexual harassment,"
he goaded.

in silence she thought
in shadows she sighed
harassment's dark whispers
men deny
year-round it haunts
a persistent fear
yet Christmas time amplifies
harsh and clear

"I'll get away with it,' he crowed.
"It's in a festive context.
A Christmas kiss.
A kiss at Christmas.
That's why there's mistletoe."

"Sexual harassment is never okay,"
the young staffer spoke up
clear as day
his response was vile
a gloating disgrace
respect and consent
should always have place

implying harassment's excusable
a dangerous game
at parties or work
it is never the same
respect and safety
should always be clear
no place for such actions
not now   not here

yet The Report claimed
with a festive defence
"How could this cause offence?"
for female staff
this logic's a dangerous call
at parties
if harassed
do not brush it off at all

festive or not

respect must be clear

no excuse

for conduct

that brings others fear

the *festive context*

makes behaviour seem okay

but it is a reminder

in a sarcastic way

everyone

beware

avoid the social spree

lest you find dignity

lost

in a rule-free melee

are we moving forward

or back

in this game

rights meant to protect

yet risked in shame

if harassment is deemed festive

we must then inspect

the integrity of justice

what does it reflect

the setting of misconduct
does not clear the blame
responsibility stands
the rules are the same
every year
we are forced to reflect
on workplace ethics
we must protect
and respect

in The Report
he bragged
with alarming glee
"I tried to kiss her."
a tale of impropriety
"She fell backwards."
his actions left their mark
in such behaviour
the darkness is stark

when questioned
he shrugged
"That's how it went."
downplaying the act
with no remorse spent
"It's just what you do," he said with a grin
but such behaviour is never a win
"It's just how it is," he downplayed the scene
"It wasn't romantic."
his actions were mean

the incidents occurred
in a *festive context*
as though the celebration
could excuse the vex
but no festivity
should mask the wrong
respect and consent
should always stay strong

in The Report
his own words did reveal
intrusive advances
unwelcome and real
toward three female staff
his actions were severe
such behaviour is a warning
women
steer clear

"I kept on resisting," Lucy did say.
he forced her head down
in a troubling way
a kiss on the forehead
unwanted and wrong
such actions are harmful
and do not belong

"He grabbed my face,"
Betty confessed with fear.
"My instinct was to freeze, as he drew near.
An out-of-body moment, a stark surreal scene."
no one
should endure
his unwanted touch or leer

He kept on asking, "Did I kiss you tonight?"
"Let me kiss you!" "No!" Desi bellowed her plight.
"I'm not interested!"
But he gripped her so tight.
"It felt impossible to break from his might."

"He fell on me. I used all my might.
To push him away,
with all my fight.
Bent back to avoid, his body on top.
Feeling trapped and helpless.
Wishing it would stop."

these testimonies
reveal trauma so deep
Lucy called it "distressing"
nights without sleep
shocked
shut in her office
colleagues gossiping every day
lingering impact
anxiety and depression sway

dismissing misconduct
unambiguous evidence
ignored
flimsy excuses over victims' rights
deplored
such actions send a message
dangerous and wrong
prioritize dignity
safety
where they belong

allowing harassment
excused by festive guise
trivializes the pain
neglects the cries
severity downplayed
workplace laws undone
safety and respect
must be for everyone

the victims' courage
shines bright and clear
their voices remind us
year after year
workplace safety
and dignity stand tall
non-negotiable rights
respected by all

anonymizing his name
shields him from his due
deprives the victims
of transparency too
actions without consequences
unjust and absurd
their right to clear justice
should always be heard

why cannot leaders
see harassment's a crime
a woman's right to say *no*
clear and prime
hiring those who exploit
power in their hand
questions arise
will values truly stand

why does this employer
let predators stay
in positions of power
workers trust
they betray
tarnishing the faith
of those they should shield
such actions leave wounds
that may never be healed

these events reminds us
how far we must tread
for meaningful reform
and safe paths ahead
workplace safety
in every space
is a non-negotiable
the only essential embrace

sexual harassment is never okay

it is all through the year

every single day

but especially at Christmas

it is clear

we must stand up

speak out

and persevere

youthfully

engagement

a youthful mind   sharp and bright   engages
in tasks day and night   learning new skills
being a social delight
it combats decline   keeping thoughts in flight
ensuring life's path remains alight
with each challenge   we ignite a mental spark
an insight   activities and skills our right
through social bonds
our hearts unite with friendship that forever delights

engagement keeps the mind so spry
sharp and agile
reaching high   against decline we never shy
in life's fullness we comply   independent
as days go by   a youthful mind
with creativity brings
innovative ideas and daring flings
in arts we find our spirit sings
challenging norms   the courage it brings
a community thrives on vibrant wings

experimenting with thoughts anew   creative arts

a vibrant hue   those conventional ways we bid adieu

innovation opens vistas true   enriching lives

for me and you   a mindset fresh with innovation's call

personal growth as we embrace it all   in vibrant culture

exhibitions we install   together we decorate every wall

a youthful mind helps keep the body free

in movement's grace   we find our key

mobility thrives longevity we see   despite

chronic disease   we declare   independence

from life's debris

youthful thoughts ignite the flame   in social bonds

we find our name engaged and active   we proclaim

a stronger sense of life's acclaim   contentment

in a shared world domain

connections built   we intertwine   in community

our spirits shine   emotional health and hearts align

belonging felt with a life online   supportive network truly mine

with active ties we find our grace   satisfaction

lights our face   relationships in warm embrace

happiness within this space

a joyful thriving community place

aging with pride in a place that's ours

L G B T Q I A+ needs met   blooming like flowers

safe and secure where love can grow

in every heart let acceptance show

going forward   our spirits rise with youthful zeal

we energize   health sometimes means compromise

longevity's gift we realize

quality of life our greatest prize   engaging in play

flirting with desire   mobility's dance can be a trip wire

an active life lifting us higher

chronic risks soon transpire

independence is our inner fire

a youthful mind with optimism's call   stress and worries

we let fall   in present moments we stand tall

proactive steps   we heed them all   mental health

improves   dealing with curve balls

youthful outlook   stress defies   anxiety fades

our strength lies in coping well when changes arise

emotional balance is our prize

through life's many shifts we find our allies

focusing now   with joyful sight   challenges faced
with hopeful might   stress reduced our hearts feel light
coping well   in day and night in later years
we might ignite
youthful thinking   vibrant glow   stress and fear
we overthrow   better mental health begins to show
in life's dance we freely flow
adjustments made as we grow

a youthful mind with resilience found
from setbacks' depths   we rebound   opportunities
for growth they are in emotional strength
so profound   mental health and well-being surround
disappointments faced   we rise anew
with youthful thoughts   we follow through
viewing growth in every view   emotional health
in what we pursue   well-being thrives in all we do

in life's setbacks   we find our stride with youthful minds
we will not hide   growth opportunities not our only guide
emotional resilience far and wide   mental health
our allies reside ever hopeful by our side

© Heather Anne Gordon
August 2022

it is not a new-fangled thing
throughout history there have been
communities   that reject
a two-gender binary thing
there are those who recognise additional genders
in a world vibrant and varied in its members
we are not singular and solitary contenders

from the revered Hijra of South Asia
so profound   to Two-Spirit people in tribes
where wisdom is found
ancient cultures knew the beauty of being
beyond rigid norms   beyond what we're seeing
in the land of Pharaohs where temples stand tall
androgynous deities were depicted in halls

two twenty-two C E – the Roman Empire's tale
Elagabalus   assassinated
a name that prevails
insisted on being called Lady
Empress of Grace
wore feminine makeup
defied norms in that place

they disguised as a female sex worker
their life a testament to gender's spectrum
from ancient Rome to today's understanding
ever expanding

in the fourteen hundreds
Eleanor Rykener's medieval plight
lived as a woman   worked day and night
arrested in thirteen ninety-four   a tale profound
as a barmaid and an embroiderer Rykener was renowned

slept with women and men both   roles varied
in a time when gender roles were heavily married
a testament to the fluidity of life
in an age defined by struggle and strife

sixteen hundreds and Thomas/Thomasine Hall's story
unfolds   raised as a girl
although a military life took glory
alternated between identities   masc and femme
Thomas and Thomasine   embraced both of them

after being arrested for having sex
with women and men both   confessed
attempts to determine their physical genitalia
intersex discovered   not fitting the social binary regalia
their story   fluidity   courageously told

felt no preference
toward either gender
expressed fluidity   before language could render
a testament to non-conformity's early embrace
in a world still learning to understand and place

seventeen to eighteen hundreds
and Britain's Molly Houses
Molly   a term reclaimed   to no one's surprise
meeting houses where gay men would gather
feminine pronouns and names
in dresses they would rather

gender non-conformity in varying degrees
expressions diverse   spanning centuries
molly houses   a sanctuary of strong defiance
in a time of strict societal
compliance

late eighteen hundreds   mid-nineteen hundreds
Jack Garland's tale   historians recovered
their story unveiled   Babe Bean was his original cover
they presented as male
in California's life   where silence prevailed
and pretences were Herculean

serving in the U S military   Jack Garland became
a male identity   with tattoos   and a new name
they worked as a nurse   in a masculine guise
lived as a man until their demise

early nineteen fifties
Christine Jorgensen's named
the first trans celebrity   media fanned the flame
surgery in nineteen fifty-two with headlines ablaze
ex- G I becomes blonde beauty   those were the days

a speaker for the trans community's plight
speaking engagements   shedding light
saying she did her own thing   for herself alone
but her journey's impact   widely known
built on history   challenging norms
living true   in all its forms

twenty twelve   Catherine McGregor
courage displayed
group captain R A A F   her path unafraid
as former lieutenant colonel   East Timor seen
announced her transition   becoming Catherine

Cate told stories of hidden transgender lives
speaking at forums where hope thrives
documented in Women's Weekly   and on T V
a beacon of bravery   for all to see

cricket commentator   author   so bold
her journey of commitment   a story of courage told
challenges faced   contentment found
inspiring others   her voice resounds

Indigenous fa'afafine in Samoa   embraced
fluidly transcending gender roles
within their space
and in the Pacific   across cultures so vast
Māhū in Hawaii and Tahiti
breaking from the binary past

not just the youth of today
but a continuum across history
a narrative enriched
far deeper than the shadows it cast
celebrating diversity that always was
always will be   as long as humanity lasts

© Heather Anne Gordon
December 2024

zestfully

august

Lily saw the social media post
for Andamooka's sala fest
determined to visit
she drove her camper van with zest
along bitumen roads
her G P S did start
to witness the sala art
that speaks to the heart

many Australians believe the arts
instil
creative skills for the future
to fulfill
essential for the workforce
yet to come
building a bright future
where ideas hum

Australians in numbers great
have come to see
how arts enrich their lives
so vibrantly
supporting and expanding minds
hearts   and souls
the arts play a vital part
making lives whole

with current focus on mental health
and social connection
we find in arts
empathy
a profound intersection
supporting minds and hearts
with creativity's direction
building stronger bonds
fostering reflection

the sustaining nature of our bonds
creativity intertwined
fostering connections
where hearts and minds align
through art and expression
we find our way
building lasting ties
in the light of each new day

art

is our soul

its beat

pure gold

yet funds are scarce

many stories   untold

politicians   heed our plea

creators need respect

as well as money

sport and art

though opposites they may seem

both shape our nation

fuelling the dream

artists   athletes

both in financial plight

prize money should not be taxed

try to set things right

when funding is divided
art gathers the crumbs
while artists struggle
full hecs still comes
athletes soar to A I S
with no financial ghosts
artists left to dream
beneath the funding posts

products judged
by cash and gold
their true worth
we leave untold
readers   viewers   listeners
starved inside
artists need support
worldwide

in August
South Australia is a powerful sight
the sala festival
in visual arts we delight
an open-access event
where creativity flows
an annual showcase
where every artist grows

the festival celebrates

with open hearts and minds

South Australian artists

where creativity binds

from young to old

each vision finds its place

in this joyful event

experience

and talent

embrace

art connects communities

inviting all to play

bringing excitement

different from the norm

each day

it educates and inspires

creativity takes the lead

uniting hearts and minds

fulfilling a multitude of need

the arts invite us
to explore and see
beyond the rules
where minds are free
with open ends
and boundless skies
they spark unique thoughts
letting creativity rise

art programs
enrich both body and mind
fostering wellbeing
of a special kind
through creativity
our spirits find relief
healing and joy
in every visual arts belief

through sensory chances
expression takes flight
inclusive for all
in both day and night
art forms unite
communication flows free
connecting us all
in shared creativity

art programs nurture
communities grow strong
encouraging exhibitions
where hearts belong
engage   reflect   and learn
experiences shared
promoting health and unity
in every path we have dared

there is a growing need
for art to thrive
in regional Australia
where traditions survive
showcasing Aboriginal forms
rich and profound
cultural heritage
in every piece found

it is crucial
for Aboriginal voices
to be heard and seen
supporting the arts
where cultures gather   serene
creating space for practices
unique and true
sharing heritage
with others
in all we do

art and culture's
expression
healing the soul
making people feel whole
their stories   told bold
through creativity   voices rise
undeterred
enabling communication
ensuring they are heard

artists weave

their magic

in social spheres

in cultural contexts

where community appears

through art events

their talents come alive

connecting hearts

and minds

where creativity thrives

Lily believes that art

with its lively hues

brings communities together

and offers

diverse views

educating on cultures

and beliefs

so profound

building bridges

between us

where common ground

is found

Lily admired
the sala show
colourful and grand
in Andamooka's
community hall
alongside the opal land
artworks told stories
capturing hearts and all
a celebration of creativity
within those
ex-Maralinga walls

artists unite
within the community
they strive
creating social change
keeping cultures alive
collaborative spirits
through art they convey.
transforming lives
in exciting
hopeful ways

with intergenerational
transfer
wisdom flows
cultural
and artistic knowledge
in hearts   it grows.
skills passed down
from old to young
a legacy of community
and art
in every exhibition hung

Lily believes
in the power of each heart
communities
and individuals
in art   to take part
pursuing brilliance
in creativity   they shine
together
they weave
a quilt   so fine

Lily knows from experience
time is the key
for connections to grow
along with
understanding to see
weeks or years
for respect and skills to blend.
in art and life
where hearts transcend

Outback Lily's zestful energy
for art's delight
and leisure's symphony
through nature's beauty
and the community's pleasure
in the exhilarating Outback
there is Australia's treasure

creativity flows
where landscapes inspire
drawing energy
from the land's eternal fire

the colours   textures   and forms
of the Outback inspire
from rich reds of the earth
to skies that never tire
in nature's wonders
innovative ideas take flight
Lily's art is born
from this electrifying light

Lily thrives on connections
within her local scene
art events and collaborations
help keep her keen
with community artists
her inspiration grows
in her community's embrace
her creativity flows

Lily respects
the traditions
wise and grand
drawing inspiration
from her vibrant land
she honours Aboriginal heritage
with a mindful heart
connecting with community
playing her own part

she continually seeks
to refine her art's grace
exploring new media
she embraces the chase
pushing creativity's bounds
ever inviting
this constant growth
keeps her practice exciting

Lily finds joy in travelling
and sharing her skills
with every story told
her passion fills
when teaching others
her heart feels alive
in building community
she strives
as her creativity
thrives

© Heather Anne Gordon
March 2024

she says

Be brave! Don't hide, let your art take flight.

Though as vulnerable as it feels, your message is right.

Visual communication lets your essence show.

Meaningful and powerful so let it grow.

In community's beauty

connections we find.

Someone out there

awaits your creative mind.

In art   we share.

Unique stories and truth.

Each voice distinct

in old age and youth.

Step forth.

Boldly.

Make your mark.

Ignite the passion.

Dispel the dark.

Your art shines brightly

a guiding spark.

© Heather Anne Gordon
April 2024

january twenty-sixth twenty twenty-five

who are we

this day
of empirical triumphalism
bunting
fireworks
and tall ships
yet trauma
and historical
near sightedness
outstrips
renowned
for neither
national self-awareness
nor reflection
a polarized celebration
without introspection

the modern Aussie state
a colonial landgrab
confounds
from genocidal roots
to sun-kissed
resistant grounds
mostly still apathetic
and defensive
about constitutional change
yet to truly
acknowledge
ancient civilisations
in its range

who are we
it is the hardy perennial
insufficiently analysed
it beams
over a divisive day
marking
a supposed birth
contentious
and marginal
demanding
a soul search
to find our true way

Australia

could be

a mature nation

with a strong sense of itself

instead

it remains

a colonial outpost

and shackled

to a would-be U S dictator

a land of potential

bound by chains

of its own creation

the need for a journey

toward

true independence

grows ever greater

instead

we cling

to archaic monarchy ties

emotionally lashed

to G B's lies

geopolitically hocked

to White House ways

no matter

which dictator's whims

it sways

our reverence

for an outdated

alliance

those ties

drawn into endless

imperial wars

under foreign skies

with Australian soil ceded

to the Pentagon's command

as a three sixty eight billion dollar Aukus deal

spins

a speculative hand

Australia

based on our ties

with Great Britain

obsequious to the U S

our ties tightly written

unquestioningly

shackled

to whims so grand

of the forty-seventh president

an unpredictable hand

will the forty-seventh invade
a N A T O ally's shore
take the Panama Canal
by military force
once more
the threats loom large
decisions remain
in the hands of the power mad
uncertainty reigns

Australia
is deeply invested
in the forty-seventh's whims
political leaders
cheer
while their own image dims
gaslighting us to chill
that alliance is the key
in the end
that is all that matters
cannot you see

it is hard to chill
to look away
or be reassured
when the richest
most powerful
with salutation
unobscured
celebrates inauguration
with echoes of the past
evoking
the Third Reich
with shadows cast

for my part
i would like a leader
or two
to call it out
reflect concerns anew
mature
beyond a colonial state
not just a blunt instrument
of the U S fate

a big part
of who we are
this modern Aussie state
celebrates today
in denial
the majority
cannot relate
to deeply racist
beginnings
and legacies
a history shadowed
with unacknowledged
tragedies

nods
to violent dispossession
and First Nations'
custodianship
they will share
but tempered
with a series of "buts"
they will prepare
acknowledgement
diluted
as history unfolds
a narrative tempered
yet truth be told

but Australia

peacefully

forged

a modern federation

yet for First Nations' peoples

it is deep frustration

immigration

egalitarianism

inclusiveness

a government claim

but the truth tells a story

of unanswered pain

but Australia

renowned for its beautiful

cities of light

civilized advances

on workers' rights

shining bright

women's suffrage

education

and voting so fair

governance admired

accomplishments

beyond compare

despite
national slogans
the truth lies stark
institutional advances
with exclusion's mark
a white federation
its foundation blocks clear
discriminating
against First Nations
instilling fear

White Australia Policy
born in nineteen oh one
reminders linger long after
the shadows long
even before that
N S W Governor's first act
appointing with care
the N S W mounted police
a force to prepare
a war against Wiradjuri
cultural lands lost
dispossession
the ultimate cost

the conflict drove its way

from Bathurst's plain

across the entire island

through dust and rain

First Nations' fight

grew far and wide

colonial forces

clashed

lands denied

a mature nation

strong in its own poise

shrugs colonial blinkers

imperial noise

dares to self-examine

past and present unfurled

seeks to find its truth

in a changing world

© Heather Anne Gordon
January 2025

colonial roots
tied to a British decree
royal influence cast
across the sea
Australia's story
steeped in royal sway
monarchical ties
remain law today

from distant shores
the Empire's call
monarchy's shadow
on cities tall
a legacy
left by royal command
Australia's history
in the monarch's hand

convicts and settlers arrived
under the crown's gaze
colonial ties
set in early days
from governors to laws
the royal hand
hemmed in our land
with the monarchical brand

a monarch's decree
laws fashioned that way
colonial roots
still present today
Australia's journey
yet in debate
monarchy's echo
shaping our fate

royal visits

pomp

and splendour grand

colonial ties

still hold the land

Australia's path

firmly under the crown

still seeking its identity

independence and renown

grow up   Australia

© Heather Anne Gordon
January 2025

lands taken
families
and cultures
torn apart
First Nations' pain
heavy heart
dispossession's shadow
long and wide
a history of sorrow
hard to hide

ancient lands
now claimed
and fenced
First Nations' voices
often silenced
hence
dispossession's tale
a wound so deep
a legacy of loss
memories we keep

from sacred grounds
to stolen earth
First Nations' pain
a story of worth
dispossession's mark
a scar that stays
echoes of the past
in present days

cultural roots
disrupted
and frayed
First Nations' pain
in history's shade
dispossession's grip
a lasting bind
seeking justice
peace of mind

grow up   Australia

© Heather Anne Gordon
January 2025

Australia's gaze
fixed
on the U S might
following their lead
day and night
geopolitical ties
a bond so tight
in the White House shadow
we seek our light

from Hollywood dreams
to military might
Australia's obsession
and constant strife
echoes of America
in our daily life
a bond unbroken
glaring
bright

U S influence

in every sphere

Australia's path

so clear

from politics to culture

we adhere

to the American way

year after year

in wars and peace

we stand aligned

Australia's fate

with the U S entwined

a partnership

deeply defined

in their shadow

our future combined

grow up   Australia

to break colonial ties
we look within
acknowledge the past
a new era begin
First Nations' voices
at the forefront stand
healing and justice
across our land

respecting
ancient cultures
their stories told
honouring the wisdom
their truths unfold
moving beyond
U S's over-reaching hand
a sovereign path
for our native land

reflecting

on our history

deeply and clear

seeking a future

that is just and near

First Nations' rights

a priority take

independence

our destiny

to embrace

reconciliation

a journey

not a race

recognizing the pain

we must face

shifting our gaze

from the U S's might

to build a nation

with its own unique light

grow up   Australia

© Heather Anne Gordon
January 2025

march eighth twenty twenty-five

"Bread and Roses"
we sing the call   fair wages and justice
for all   women striving   dignity their quest
bread for survival   roses for rest

from street protests   to boardroom sway
have we lost touch   with March eighth's day
remembering our roots   the activism and fights
honouring those who paved   the path to our rights

marching together   collaborating
not always with equal stride   feminists
worldwide   with hearts open wide
championing rights   to have a say
they have worked their way
to International Women's Day
we shout hooray

seventeen eighty-eight
Britain's cold grasp
on gender roles   brought
convicts   to harsh lands
women's freedoms   fraught
bound to men's pockets
without rights   or say
they braved the storms
in a life bleak and grey
Australia's suffragists   collaborated
for women's rights they set the stage

eighteen forty-eight
Elizabeth Cady Stanton
Lucretia Mott
Mary McClintock
Martha Coffin Wright
Jane Hunt
in U S A's Seneca Falls
where Stanton spoke
a call for change and justice broke
Sentiments declared the start of the fight
for equal laws and women's rights

eighteen fifty-seven

New York City

in March eight's light

textile workers   in a tireless fight

for shorter days and decent pay

their voices soared on that brave day

eighteen ninety-three

New Zealand

led the world

with its bold decision

women   gained the vote

in a national election vision

on nineteenth September equality took its stance

a historic move   giving progress for women

a chance

eighteen ninety-four

South Australia

after ten years

of struggle on the eighteenth of December

women secured a milestone to remember

votes and seats   in Parliament

their rights were unfurled

equality in politics   a first in the world

Mary Lee
Mary Colton
Catherine Helen Spence
in a world where women strove
against entrenched views
their courage showed
letters   speeches   rallies set the tone
a four hundred feet long petition
making their determination known

nineteen hundred and nine
Theresa Malkiel
from U S A's National Women's Day
I W D's roots spread globally
February twenty-eighth
for worker's fair pay   challenging suffrage
they led the way

nineteen ten
Luise Zietz and Clara Zetkin
in Copenhagen's hall
stood strong
declared the day to belong
March eighth for women   a day of their might
united for justice   and for their rights

nineteen eleven

on nineteenth March

they took a stand

in Germany   Australia   Denmark

Switzerland

one million strong   both women and men

International Women's Day   began

nineteen twelve

Helen Todd

her speech ignited the fire

bread and roses   their hearts' desire

textile workers   women and young

protested loudly   with voices strong

nineteen thirteen

U K's Epsom Derby

Emily Davison   suffragette

fierce and bold   ran onto the track

died three days later her story   widely known

nine arrests   seven hunger strikes

in prison life   force-fed forty-nine times

pursuing votes for women's rights

Emily died for the right to vote

remember Emily when you enrol to vote

nineteen fourteen

Sylvia Pankhurst

in front of Charing Cross

stood defiant and proud

arrested enroute   voice still loud

from Bow to Trafalgar the march was grand

for women's suffrage they took a stand

nineteen seventeen

on March the eighth

in Petrograd so grand

women marched   with strength

took a bold stand   for bread and roses

their spirits untamed   a revolution sparked

their courage proclaimed

nineteen twenty

Susan B Anthony

Elizabeth Cody Stanton

others working together

after seventy-two years the vote's in sight

the nineteenth Amendment U S A's history's quote

women were 'granted'   the right to vote

despite the ink on paper

poor women   and women of colour

their right to vote

remained a distant   dream deep

into the twentieth century's stream

nineteen twenty-one

at the Second Internationale

Russia chose the date

to honour women's roles in Russia's fate

I W D stands a symbol bright

against exploitation   pro workers' rights

nineteen twenty-two

China   Uzbekistan   Turkmenistan's cheer

with Tajikistan   marks I W D each year

with pride and honour their voices unite

     celebrating women

nineteen twenty-eight

Edna Ryan

in Sydney's Domain   on March twenty-fifth

began the campaign when I W D reached

Australia's shore

women's voices united   demanding more

nineteen twenty-nine

Jessie Street

diplomat   suffragette

campaigner for Indigenous Australian rights

led the charge with pride

United Associations of Women

stood side by side   I W D committees across the land

bringing diverse voices   hand in hand

nineteen thirty-one

in the heart of Sydney

and in Melbourne's streets wide

women raised banners   their voices amplified

from soapbox stands   their messages flowed

across the nation   their courage showed

Newcastle's streets   echoed their song

Wollongong joined in   their spirits strong

Ipswich stood firm   no justice denied

united they marched   with hope as their guide

while white men   met in numbers

by the soapbox   to hear

and trade unions   dominated by men

made it clear

the women's movement stood

labelled middle-class

a divide in voices   a struggle to surpass

nineteen thirty-five

Anna Morgan

led with heartfelt plea

Australian Aborigines' League

in January   to the Minister for Interior

for Aboriginal women   education   their fight

a delegation united   seeking their right

nineteen thirty-seven

in Sydney

two hundred women strong

women's voices   in speeches long

world peace they sought   with earnest plea

a foremost concern   for all to see

nineteen forty-two
in Ipswich   women gathered
funds to raise for the Red Cross
their unity praised   allied women united
determined to stand   defeating Fascism
hand in hand

nineteen fifties
Cold War tensions and lines were drawn
women's unity tested before the dawn
radical voices sidelined   yet strong
in activism's tale they definitely belong

nineteen sixties and nineteen seventies
anti-communist sentiment high
I W D organizers reached for the sky
for peace   equal pay   Aboriginal rights
struggling to find venues facing tough fights

Australian women   persisted
their spirits high   hosting visitors
under a common sky
from China   Indonesia   Vietnam
Soviet Union's might   the strength
of women's bonds shining bright

nineteen seventy-two

women marched with a cause

determined and fierce

against gender injustice

their mission was clear

Aboriginal rights   contraception

abortion   and ending the strife

of domestic violence   fighting for every life

nineteen seventy-four

Anne Summers   Jennifer Dakers   Bessie Guthrie

on March sixteenth   fuelled by an I W D forum

equipped   with brooms and shovels

without decorum   through the night they worked

passion alight   two vacant homes claimed

their stance was right

Elsie Women's Refuge a beacon of might

nineteen seventy-eight

Aileen Moreton-Robinson

unveiled the power   hidden

the privilege   unspoken

with Goenpul insight the silence was broken

in Australia's feminism her revelations unfurled

a unique voice in the global feminist world

nineteen eighties

street protests dwindle drowned by corporate sheen

I W D co-opted   true voices unseen

catch phrases shine but demands they miss

the call for change we cannot dismiss

twenty eighteen

Celeste Liddle   Arrente woman   unionist

exposing I W D's whitewashed guise

where companies exploit and justice cries

a call to action not just catchy lines

Aboriginal women fight   on multiple frontlines

twenty twenty-one

March4Justice showed the fire

still burns   bright against gendered wrongs

they rise to the fight   energized and ready

they fill the streets protesting for change

where justice meets

twenty twenty-four

Megan Davis   Cobble Cobble woman

professor of law with insight so keen

calls out the elites for the gaps in between

First Nations voices their struggles revealed

a united call for justice   their wounds to be healed

twenty twenty-five
International Women's Day
has dulled its fervent cry
slogans   replace the spirit
of days gone by   revolution's edge
now lost in the haze true meaning buried
in a catch phrase maze

are we singing   for peace and bread
or breakfast   with platitudes fed
do we march   with purpose ahead
or leave our ideals gathering dust
on a neglected bookshelf   instead

© Heather Anne Gordon
January 2025

men can be allies it is true
speaking out against sexism
it is up to you   men   start confronting those jokes
and actions unkind   start promoting equality
leaving stereotypes behind

systemic advantages deeply ingrained
listening to women's stories no longer constrained
taking a stand   educating your minds
building a future where justice aligns

amplifying
women's voices   not taking their place
crediting their ideas   in every space   challenging sexism
not letting it slide   speaking out against it
with courage and pride

uplifting

women's leadership

in all we do   fostering growth

each day anew   sharing

domestic tasks

not just *lending a helping hand*

taking full responsibility together we stand

empowering one another every woman we see

because strong women create

a strong community

thinking

about your words and what they convey

treating women with respect every day

supporting women's rights

donating your time   promoting

gender equality   it is about time

checking

your privilege   reflecting and see

how it influences your life and how it can be

men have advantages in many systemic ways

you can help change the system for future days

being open

to feedback and willing to learn

being proud to be an ally   it is your turn

your support is vital in this fight

for gender equality let us do what's right

because

men earn more and are promoted higher

it is often told   even though women

strive equally yet lag in roles

qualifications match   experience too

breaking these barriers is long overdue

in politics

men still dominate the stage

women fight for seats

to turn the page   systems lacking

their voices restrained   equality sought

representation gained

social expectations

women's time takes shape with family and obligations

men often escape while women juggle roles

on their shoulders rest responsibilities

it is time for balance and shared roles to manifest

walking home solo men often at ease
women feel danger their caution increased
harassment and fear a night's silent dread
seeking a world where all can tread
without fear

home life's
demands   women often bear
their time and growth caught in this snare
career aspirations opportunities slim
striving for balance let equality win

healthcare access
men often fare well   women's needs
sidelined   stories to tell
reproductive rights funding gaps clear
striving for equity   health without fear

media spotlight
men bask in the glow women in stereotypes
their worth to show   ageism entwined
stories unfold challenging biases
let truth be told

in education
women excel while breaking the mould
in every classroom their stories unfold
achievements shine as barriers fall
education empowers   uplifting all

women advance
yet men often prevail
this is where opportunities sometimes derail
disparities linger in resources and chance
striving for balance in every advance

men's voices
roar
women's often missed
men age as silver foxes women dismissed
bias runs deep unfairly told
striving for respect both young and old

men's systemic gains
fairness we apply when sharing the pie
no one is denied   there is more for all
as equity draws near
together we thrive
with nothing to fear

© Heather Anne Gordon
February 2025

acknowledgement of country

The arrival of Europeans in South Australia had an indelible impact on the First Nations people who lived here prior to 1837.

Significantly, unlike the rest of Australia, South Australia was not considered to be terra nullius ("nobody's land") upon the arrival of Europeans.

When the fledgling province of South Australia was established by the South Australia Act 1834, the subsequent Letters Patent expressly acknowledged prior Aboriginal ownership of the land and stated that no actions could be undertaken that would

"affect the rights of any Aboriginal Natives… to the actual occupation or enjoyment in their own Persons or in the Persons of their Descendants of any Lands therein now actually occupied or enjoyed by such Natives."

Nonetheless, under the Act, the Aboriginal owners of the land were deemed to have become British subjects and while the Letters Patent guaranteed – on paper - land rights for the First Nations people, in practice these provisions were ignored by the South Australia Company specifically and the white colonists more broadly.

Massacres (by definition the deliberate killing of six or more relatively undefended people in one operation) have been reported and mapped.

The South Australian parliament was established in 1857. When women in South Australia gained the right to vote in 1894, it included Aboriginal women. At the Ngarrindjeri mission, a number of Aboriginal women insisted on enrolling on the electoral roll and voting in the 1896 election. South Australia was the first colony in Australia and only the fourth place in the world where women gained the vote.

South Australia took a national lead in land rights legislation with the passage of the Aboriginal Lands Trust Act in 1966.

South Australia was the first state in Australia to enact Aboriginal land rights legislation with the Pitjantjatjara Land Rights Act initiated by the Dunstan Labor government passed in 1981 in modified form by the Liberal government of David Tonkin. The Maralinga-Tjarutja Land Rights Act was passed in 1984.

The recognition of Native Title came in 1992 with the High Court's decision in Mabo.

Acknowledging Country is an opportunity to remind us of the whole history of our country.

It reminds us that we are a nation of many layers from the most ancient to the most recent. It reminds us that we, as Australians, have an amazing gift. It is the gift that Aboriginal people through survival and custodianship of the country provide to the nation.

That is, the most ancient and oldest continuing population on the planet. That is extremely powerful and is fundamental to the identity of this nation.

It reminds us of the unfinished business of our nation. That is, the lack of equitable social justice outcomes for First Nations People.

Think of Aboriginal people's use of technologies for tools and weaving, art, knowledge of medicinal plants, stories of the night sky, travels for trading and cultural events.

Kokatha, Barngarla, Kuyani, Adnyamathanha Country:
Andamooka area
Ngadjuri, Peramangk, Kaurna Country:
Barossa Valley region
South Australia

first readers and research friends

As a writer, I don't write alone. My writing is with other people's voices in my head, the media cycle alarming me, the need to talk things through.

Thank you, First Readers, for Outback Lily

Alison Smoker	reflectively
Andrea Hoffmann	morally
Bec Huchins	exceptionally
Beck Hanold	therapeutically
Brenda Murray	gracefully
Danette Oughton	xmessily
Deb Lindner	judgementally
Deb Selway	youthfully
Debbie Warren	bravely, ultimately
Donna Waters	obliviously
Elizabeth Schulz	quixotically
Gayle Mather	deliberately, january twenty-sixth
Jena Jaensch	flourishingly, hopefully
Julie King	naughtily
Liney Deer	kaleidoscopically
Mary Ames	ideally
Melanie Carter	sanctimoniously, verbally, zestfully, march eighth
Olivia Newell	whisperingly
Robyne Lesley	allegedly, consequently, plausibly
The Shaz	legislatively

first readers   companions in creation
their feedback   a beacon of delight
invisible networks   threads of love
voices that lift me   lifelines of grace

Each episode of Outback Lily was originally published in digital format as free downloads available from www.heathergordon.com.au during February 2025.

that first draft

Some understand the courage, and the vulnerability, required to share a first draft. First readers are the first to see the writing as it truly is: raw, unfinished, brimming with possibility and peril. They are the ones who encourage me.

These early readers give me more than feedback. They offer companionship in the isolating process of creation, and their support is a bollard against the tides of self-doubt.

Behind many of the details in my stories is a network of generous friends. Their patience is limitless; their curiosity contagious; their willingness to travel to a location and discuss plotlines invaluable.

The listeners: those who sit with me at my kitchen table or around the campfire and let me spin variations of plot, character arcs, and motivations. They are the sounding boards for my wildest ideas. Sometimes, they fall in love with my characters even more fiercely than I do, and their passion reinvigorates my own.

Every draft, every episode, is the product of invisible networks: of love, encouragement, and critical insight.

These networks are not merely support systems of generosity; they are lifelines. They link me to people I might never otherwise have met, people who believe in the power of story and the worthiness of voices. Mine included. They hold me up when medical appointments take all day and I'm exhausted by pain and the next day is lost to recovery.

To publish my own voice is, in the end, an act of both humility and courage. While my stories are uniquely mine, I am shaped by every voice that has ever reached out to me: whether in critique, encouragement, argument or shared enthusiasm.

I want to write stories that ring true. Not because they echo other voices, but because they bear the imprint of every person who has helped me see more clearly. As I fling these words into the world, I am grateful for those who lend their ears, their eyes, and their hearts.

Heather Anne Gordon August 2025 www.heathergordon.com.au